Chance's Return

by

Lucy Naylor Kubash

North Star Legacy

Publishing History
First Edition, 2025
Trade Paperback ISBN 978-1-5092-6078-2
Digital ISBN 978-1-5092-6079-9

North Star Legacy
Published in the United States of America

Dedication

Dedicated to the Grand Teton Mountains of Wyoming, where the seeds for this story and those to follow were first planted in my brain.

Chapter 1

Chance McCord tipped back his hat with a thumb and lifted his weary gaze to the mountains ahead. He set his saddle on the roadside to take a moment's break from walking. In the past half hour, storm clouds had amassed over the Tetons, staining the sky a violent shade of purple. Thunder rolled across the valley, setting a nearby bunch of Angus steers to lowing and a jackrabbit scurrying for cover. In a minute, it would pour buckets.

Chance didn't mind the rain. The stretch of northwest Wyoming highway shimmered under a sun that burned mighty hot and dry for this early in the summer, and he would welcome a rush of cool mountain air right about now. He just hated for his saddle to get wet. A fine cutting saddle, it was a parting gift from his buddy Hank. Since the truck broke down outside of Boulder, one of the few possessions of any value Chance had left in the world.

He'd thumbed the rest of the way and wished now he hadn't asked the semi driver to let him out ten miles back. Did he think walking would make things easier? Give him more time to think about what he faced? He'd had plenty of time to think—five long years—and nothing in his mind had changed. Maybe walking was a form of retribution…a way to make amends.

In truth, he was just putting off the inevitable. He

reached into his shirt pocket, drawing out a tattered photograph. He always carried it with him right over his heart. As he studied the photo now, a memory pierced him so swift it took his breath away. Lately, those memories had begun to fade, taking away some of the pain, but today, he held onto the pain so he wouldn't forget.

Thunder rumbled again, and he slipped the photo back into its place, making sure his dusty denim jacket covered it. He lifted the saddle and rested it against his hip. The town of Jackson lay ahead. He could sit out the storm there, but he'd never make it in time to beat the rain. Storms blew fast out of the mountains, and this one wasn't wasting any time. The wind picked up and sent a scraggly tumbleweed skittering across the pavement. Chance raised his face to feel the breath of the mountains on his damp brow. Then, with a heavy sigh, he pulled the brim of his cowboy hat low over his forehead, shifted the weight of the saddle, slung his duffle over his shoulder, and prepared to be drenched.

****

Casey frowned and swung the pickup truck into the only available parking space outside the line of busy shops. A swarm of tourists jam-packed the town today, but that wasn't the reason for her concern. In the last half hour, the clear Wyoming sky had grown murky as mounting rain clouds swept down the Tetons. Soon, they would let loose their fury on the streets of Jackson.

The folks thronging the sidewalks of the valley town cast glances to the mountains. When a jag of sulfur-yellow lightning snaked above the peaks, they hurried inside the nearest shops and restaurants.

"I think we better make a run for it, too, or we're

going to get soaked." She glanced at the small boy sitting across from her on the truck seat. Dressed in a red plaid shirt, jeans, and a straw cowboy hat, seven-year-old Jamie was the picture of a pint-sized wrangler. Casey sighed, her mind easing to see the healthy color of his skin and the eager light in his eyes. He looked so much better than when they'd come to Wyoming three weeks ago. She didn't want to jeopardize that fact by letting him get wet and chilled. "Too bad we didn't think to bring our rain slickers."

"But the sun was shining when we left the ranch." Jamie pressed his nose against the truck window and studied the approaching storm. "How could it change so fast?"

"Guess that's just Wyoming." Casey quickly ushered him from the pickup into the nearby crowded Book Corral. "You remember what Kyle said—if you don't like the weather here, just wait a minute. It'll change. Looks like he was right."

Just as the glass door eased shut behind them, a gust of wind sent clouds of dust swirling down the sidewalk. Seconds later, huge drops of rain spattered the store window.

"Whew, just in time, Mom." Jamie grinned from beneath the hat's brim.

"You've got that right." Casey squeezed the boy's shoulder, then steered him to the children's corner in the rear of the store. They took their time choosing several easy reader books. After she settled him at a child-size table to flip through them, Casey turned to finding a book for herself.

For its small size, the Book Corral offered a wide variety of books, ranging from mystery and science fiction to romance and poetry. As a librarian, Casey spent a lot of time reading, but she never tired of searching for a new favorite author. Matt had often laughed at her ability to "bury her nose in a book and shut out the world."

But the truth was, in the past two years, she couldn't shut out a world suddenly turned upside down, and reading for fun had taken a far back seat to just learning to get on with life. Coming to Wyoming was a big step in that direction, and now, she needed to do some of the things she'd once enjoyed.

Matt would want it that way.

She chose the latest bestseller by her favorite mystery writer and a collection of short stories and verse by various western authors. Learning more about the West while they were here couldn't hurt. Casey rounded up her son and paid the cashier for the books, but the rain still pelted down in driving sheets. Thunder rumbled overhead, and Jamie's hand crept into hers.

"What're we gonna do, Mom?"

Casey chewed her bottom lip and thought a minute. "I don't like the idea of driving back in this. Maybe we should just sit it out for a while." She wasn't used to driving the long stretches of Wyoming highway and would never have started out if she'd known the weather would change so rapidly. She should have checked the weather app on her phone.

They'd ventured into town alone for the first time today. Every other time, Aunt Billie had accompanied them, but if she and Jamie were spending the whole summer here, sooner or later they had to get around on their own.

"But I'm thirsty, Mom." Jamie peered out the

foggy shop window. "Can't we get something to drink?"

Back home, the big chain bookstore where they shopped boasted its own refreshment corner. This bookstore was totally dedicated to books.

"The Hitching Post is close by," another customer offered. "Coffee's not bad."

"Can we go there?" Jamie rubbed his nose. "I'm kind of hungry, too."

Casey contemplated the sheet of gray rain blowing down the street, then her son's small face. "I suppose we could make a dash for it." She pulled Jamie's hat down snug on his head. "Ready? Okay, hang onto your books, buddy, and let's go."

Clutching their packages, they sprinted to the café two doors down and hurried inside. Casey glanced about the bustling Hitching Post. A lot of other folks had the same idea.

Dishes clattered and voices were raised as the overwhelmed servers filled orders for the mob of tourists that, with the advent of the storm, had descended on them.

Casey didn't see a single empty table or booth.

"Room only at the counter, honey." A harried server jerked her head toward the lunch counter.

Casey saw the two empty seats, one on either side of a tall, broad-shouldered man. His hat and faded denim jacket said *cowboy*, and he looked intimidating, even with his back turned.

She was reluctant to ask him to move over, but being on her own had forced her to fend for herself and do things she never thought she'd have to do. With only a second's hesitation, Casey marched up to the counter and smiled. "Could you please move down one? All the other seats are taken."

For a minute, she didn't think he'd heard. He remained hunched over the full-to-the-brim mug of coffee that sat steaming on the counter in front of him. He hadn't made it to the café in time to avoid the downpour. Rain darkened the faded denim jacket, and his battered, equally wet, black cowboy hat tilted low over his forehead, shadowing his face. He seemed totally withdrawn from the bustle of the café around him.

Casey cleared her throat to speak again and found herself looking into eyes the same color as the moody sky above the mountains. With the chary gaze of a lone wolf, the man stared from beneath the hat brim. He needed a shave, and his dark hair curled just above the collar of his jacket. In one glance, he took her all in, from her pink running shoes and skinny jeans to her green-and-white college sweatshirt. His gaze lifted and dwelled on her face. She shifted from one foot to the other. A crazy rush of warmth flooded her from her toes to the roots of her ponytailed hair.

"Hey, can we sit down?" Jamie asked. "I'm really hungry."

The fact he'd eaten lunch only a few hours ago didn't seem to matter. Lately, Jamie was hungry all the time.

The boy's remark did the trick.

A smile crinkled the man's tanned face. "Sure enough, partner." He stood just long enough to hoist himself over to the next stool.

Jamie scrambled up beside him.

The man pulled the brim of the boy's hat down

over his wavy blond hair.

Scrunching his nose, Jamie tipped his head back and gave the stranger the once-over. "You a cowboy, mister?"

Casey poked her son. "Jamie, hush. Don't ask a bunch of questions now." In three weeks' time, Jamie had also lost a lot of his bashfulness. Simply too many people lived at the North Star ranch, and too much happened for him to remain shy for long. But no doubt this guy wouldn't appreciate a kid's questions. When it came to cowboys, Jamie was an avid fan, and anybody who dressed like one became instant hero material. Despite his friendly gesture, this particular cowboy didn't look interested in being a little boy's hero.

"It's okay, ma'am. I don't mind." He winked at her.

That sort of masculine wink could do strange things to one's equilibrium. Casey snatched the plastic-covered menu and stared at it, although, unlike Jamie, she wasn't a bit hungry.

"I guess you could say I'm a cowboy," the man told a rapt Jamie. "I work the ranches and chase cattle for a living. Do you think I qualify?"

Jamie grinned and nodded. "What kind of horse do you have? Is it a palo...palo?"

Several moments passed, and then the cowboy shook his head. "Palomino? No, no palomino. I used to have a horse named Smoky. I haven't seen him in a long time."

"What kind of horse?" Jamie wiggled on the round stool and pushed his hat back up on his head.

"Smoky was an Appaloosa. I raised him from a colt. I did ride a palomino once or twice in the rodeo."

"You mean you're in the rodeo?" Jamie stared at the cowboy. "Mom read me a story about a rodeo cowboy who won lots of big fancy buckles. How many did you win?"

"Jamie, that's enough," Casey admonished. "I thought you were hungry."

"I am." He leaned over to study the menu she held. "I'll have two tacos and a root beer." He eyed Casey.

"I hope you can eat it all." Relieved to have Jamie eating well again, she hated to deny him. For too long after Matt had died, her son had lost interest in everything. Then he'd had a bout with strep throat last winter that left him weak and unable to eat much more than broth and crackers for a few weeks.

The server stopped by them.

Casey ordered the tacos and root beer for Jamie and a cup of tea for herself. While she waited for the food to arrive, she slipped one of the books from its bag and opened it to read the inside cover.

"You'll enjoy it," the man said.

She glanced up to find him watching her again.

He nodded toward the book. "Those authors write excellent stories about the West."

His admittance of following the rodeo circuit and working the ranches, not to mention his rugged and weatherworn appearance, suggested the kind of man who spent most of his life working outdoors, rather than inside reading. The remark piqued Casey's curiosity. "Have you read them all?" She scrutinized the man's tanned face, the tiny squint lines at the corners of his eyes, and the deep grooves carved around his mouth. By his looks, he'd spent a lifetime exposed to the harsh elements of wind and sun. He just didn't seem the type who sat still long enough to read a book.

"Most of my time is spent chasing after hard-headed cows. But winter nights are long, and a good book can be a man's best friend, no matter who you are."

That's what she got for stereotyping the man. After all, having met Justin McCord, she should have known that most western men didn't fit the roughneck image held by many people. A successful rancher in the Buffalo River Valley, Justin owned an extensive library on the American West and, since his illness, had spent most of his time recording the history of his own family in the valley. "I'm sorry," Casey said. "I didn't mean that the way it sounded. Are you from around here?"

His dark blue gaze remained fixed on her face a moment before he dipped his head and took a swallow of coffee. "Originally. Been a while since I've traveled this far north." He set the cup down and stared into its black depths. A frown plowed a deep furrow between his thick brows. "I've been in southern Colorado mostly, but I travel around a lot."

One of those itinerant cowboys Justin had talked about. The kind who drifted from one rodeo, one ranch to another, working day jobs and the roundups and never putting down roots anywhere. Pity he didn't have a place to call home.

Their order came, and she busied herself tucking a napkin under Jamie's chin so he wouldn't dribble taco sauce on his new shirt. She poured a smidgen of cream into her tea and took several sips.

"You and your family vacationing in Jackson Hole?" The cowboy leaned his arms on the counter and watched Jamie put away the first taco with no effort.

"Jamie and I are a family." Casey could finally admit it without hurting so much. "And actually, I'm working here for the summer on a ranch."

His brows peaked.

At five-foot-three and barely a hundred and ten pounds, Casey hardly looked the type to wrangle cows, although many women did just that.

"My mom's helping cook for the ranch hands," Jamie piped up. "She's gonna write a book. But most of the time, she's a librarian. We live in Michigan."

At her son's unabashed bragging, Casey flushed and pointed to the other taco on his plate. "Finish everything and never mind."

"That sounds impressive. Librarians have my respect. How do you find that job?"

Was he interested in what she had to say? Casey fiddled with the teacup. "I enjoy it, but sometimes it's a challenge to convince kids and even adults that reading is still a worthwhile activity. Books have a lot of competition with social media, smart phones, and video games, to mention just a few distractions."

"Why improve your mind when you can rot it out?"

Casey glanced up and noticed wry amusement dancing in the man's eyes. He had a sense of humor after all. "Something like that. I have nothing against those things. I just believe reading expands our worlds in many ways."

He considered this, then tipped his hat back a little with his thumb. "So, tell me. What is a librarian from Michigan doing working on a ranch in Wyoming?"

Her story sounded contradictory, as much as his own interest in reading. How could she explain why they were in Wyoming? "We came out to visit my late husband's aunt. She's worked on the ranch for a long time, but she lost her husband this past winter, and she's feeling lonely. When I received her invitation to spend the summer here, I asked for a leave of absence from my library. I've been helping with the cooking, too."

"Tell him about the book, Mom." Jamie stuffed a bite of taco in his mouth.

Casey dipped her head to hide the heat on her cheeks. "I'm sure he doesn't want to hear about that." She hoped the stranger had not taken note of Jamie's remark.

"Sure I do," the cowboy said. "Let me guess, you write romance novels on the side."

She bristled a little at his tone, because she did like to read them and shook her head. "It's not even my book. The owner of the ranch where I'm staying discovered I'm a librarian, and he asked if I would help him catalog some old documents and a journal about his family's role in settling the valley. I'm just helping him enter information into the computer. He hopes to put it all in a book and have it published to hand down to his son."

"That's mighty nice of you." He rubbed one hand over his whiskery chin. "The history of the valley is pretty colorful. Do you like history?"

Casey shrugged. "I do, and it's fun helping him. He's an older gentleman who's been ill. He wants to pay me for the work, but letting Jamie and me stay at the North Star for the summer is payment enough."

The man froze, his hand stopped halfway to lifting the coffee cup to his mouth. Slowly, he set the cup down and peered at her. "You're staying at Justin McCord's place?"

Surprised, Casey gave a tentative nod. "Do you know him?"

Several seconds passed.

The cowboy placed his hands flat on the counter in front of him. "You said he's been ill. Is it anything serious?"

How much should she reveal to this stranger? His rigid posture showed genuine concern, and his voice sounded thick with tension. Perhaps at one time, he had worked for Justin McCord at the North Star. "I understand he suffered a heart attack this past spring, and the doctor advised him to slow down. He's had to turn most of the ranch business over to his son, and that's not easy for him. I guess that's why writing the book has become so important. It keeps him from fretting over the things he can't do. Aunt Billie says since I started working on the project, Justin is feeling much better."

"Billie's your aunt? And you say Sam died last winter?"

"Yes," Casey whispered.

"I didn't know." He snatched off his hat and dropped it on the counter. He raked rough fingers through his hair, rumpling up the crisp dark waves that grew back from his forehead.

Casey noticed the sprinkling of lighter hairs that silvered the ebony ones. Once more, a peculiar sympathy for the stranger rushed through her. What she'd told him was tearing him apart. "How is it you know Billie?" she asked gently. "And Justin McCord?"

He put his hands over his face and remained very

still.

Puckering up his face, Jamie glanced from the big man beside him to Casey.

She lifted a finger to her lips for the boy to keep silent.

When the cowboy glanced at them again, his eyes glistened. He pressed his fingers over them, then grabbed his hat, jamming it on and jerking the brim low over his forehead.

"I suppose you could say I know them." He let out a long sigh and clasped his hands about the cooling coffee cup. "Justin is my father. I'm Chance McCord, the prodigal son of the North Star Ranch."

Chapter 2

Casey's mouth fell open. No one, not even Aunt Billie, had spoken about another McCord son. Casey had simply taken it for granted Kyle was Justin's only child. But if what this cowboy said was true and he was also Justin's son, then where had he been this whole time? He didn't even know about Sam Murphy's passing.

Chance glanced at Casey. "Don't look so shocked. I'm sure none of my family talks about me, but I was born and raised on the North Star. Billie was like my second mother. Sam was our best hand...and my best friend. How...did he die?"

Heartfelt grief lay etched on his face. She could at least explain the events surrounding the tragedy. "Last December, there was a bad storm brewing. Sam went out to take hay to the cattle in the feed ground. He was supposed to wait for Kyle and Justin to come back from town and help toss bales from the wagon. Billie said Sam was a stubborn man, insisted on doing things himself. Somehow, the tractor tipped over. Kyle found him when they came home."

Chance's mouth tugged up in a half-smile, and he shook his head. "That was Sam, all right. Stubborn old cuss. Thought he knew it all, and he usually did. He was Justin's right hand, but he saved my butt many times. I sure appreciated Sam running interference with my father."

Casey had the feeling Justin and Chance had not always seen eye to eye. Maybe the reason for the estrangement and the younger McCord's leaving but why no communication? He didn't even know of his father's illness. "Didn't anyone tell you about all of this? I mean, if you and Aunt Billie were close, why didn't she let you know? And your brother didn't tell you your father was—"

"It's not their fault," Chance broke in. He downed the rest of his tepid coffee. "I haven't had any contact with my family in five years. They had no idea where to find me."

Her own family back in Michigan had their issues, but Casey had a hard time understanding his casual mention of an estrangement. She couldn't imagine her brother leaving and not being in touch for years. "But somebody could've died while you were gone." She instantly regretted her careless remark. Somebody *had* died, and the pain and remorse that tightened Chance McCord's jaw told her he would never forgive himself for not having been here. "I'm sorry. I didn't mean to make bad news worse."

Chance waved away her apology and bowed his head for a moment, rubbing at the frown between his brows with two fingers. He glanced up. "How is Billie doing? Somehow, I just can't think of her without Sam. Those two were a pair."

Casey recalled the time Sam and Billie came to Michigan, loaded with presents for Jamie. They were the first to call Casey after Matt's plane went down, and their messages of sympathy and encouragement in the following months were of great solace. "From what I

15

remember, they liked to spar a lot, but they loved each other. Aunt Billie misses him terribly, but she's pretty strong and believes that life goes on."

The man's deep-blue gaze met Casey's. "Does it?" He swiveled away and stared out the window of the café.

The storm abated. It was time to leave.

"Are you finished?" She pushed her empty cup away and wiped Jamie's face with his crumpled napkin. "We should get back. Aunt Billie will send Kyle out to look for us, and I'm sure he has more important things to do." She gathered up their packages. Chance still stared out the window, his back and shoulders taut with tension. Was he on his way home to the North Star or just passing through when the storm hit?

"Is he coming, too, Mom?" Jamie slid off the stool and glanced back at the man who was so friendly for a while. "Does he really know Aunt Billie? Why'd he go away?"

Casey sighed at her son's inquisitiveness. She should have known he was hanging on their every word. Yet, she couldn't reprimand him. Not for anything did she want Jamie to go back to the troubled little boy of such a short time ago. She focused on him. "Yes, Jamie, he knows Aunt Billie, but I don't think it's any of our business what happened."

Jamie scuffed the toe of one boot over the other and stared down at his feet. "I was just askin'." He shrugged.

"I know." Casey chucked his small chin up to make him look at her. "But asking questions is one thing. Being nosy is another." She smiled to let him know his mistake was a minor one and easily forgiven.

The server dropped Casey's bill on the counter. "You folks come back again."

Before she made her way to the cashier, Casey saw the girl hold the coffeepot poised above Chance's cup.

"Care for anymore, cowboy?" Her pert young face glowed with plenty of interest in his tall, rugged physique, and she was not at all shy about letting him know it.

She's wasting her effort on this man.

Roused, Chance turned and covered the cup with the palm of one hand. "No, thanks." He rose stiffly from the counter and reached into the pocket of his faded jeans. Extracting a wadded up five-dollar bill, he smoothed it out a bit and laid it carefully next to his cup. "Keep the change." He bent to retrieve a canvas duffel bag that lay slumped on the floor beneath the counter.

"Will you be back around?" The girl grabbed the bill but leaned on the counter toward him.

"Hard to tell," he murmured.

Casey hurried to pay her check. There was no sign of Chance outside the cafe, but as she and Jamie reached their parking space, she spotted him standing on the sidewalk, duffel bag slung over his shoulder, a heavy western saddle gripped in one hand. She'd glimpsed the saddle leaning up against the building, out of the rain, when they'd first entered the Hitching Post.

She met his gaze. His stormy blue eyes turned a shade softer in the natural light.

He jerked his head toward the pickup with the five-pointed star on its door. "I don't suppose you'd consider giving a cowboy a lift, would you?"

She wasn't in the habit of giving complete

strangers a ride, but Chance McCord could hardly count as that. He was Justin's son and, evidently, he was going home. "I'd be glad to." She paused to dig around in her shoulder bag for the elusive keys. "If you don't mind my slowpoke driving. I'm not too good at handling a stick shift. I'd never even driven one until we came here, but that seems the only kind of vehicle they have on the ranch."

Chance lifted the door of the truck cap and hoisted the saddle and duffel bag inside. In a halting gait, he walked to the passenger side of the truck and took some time folding his tall frame into the cab.

Jamie scrambled in on the driver side, wiggling with excitement.

"Buckle up." Casey pointed to his seat belt. She slid behind the wheel. "Aunt Billie wouldn't teach me to drive a stick. Said she's too old to give driving lessons and appointed one of the wranglers at the ranch to show me how to drive the truck. Roy persevered, but I'm afraid I wasn't a very adept student. I'm still a little klutzy about meshing the clutch with the brake."

Casey's senses hummed from the man's presence in the truck cab. He overwhelmed the limited space, but something more made her hesitate before turning the key. Would she make a fool of herself and forget everything Roy had so patiently taught her about driving the temperamental truck?

He caught her gaze as it flickered toward him. "Something wrong?"

Determined he shouldn't affect her this way, Casey shook her head. "No, of course not. It's just..." She took in his cramped posture again. The corners of his mouth pinched with a vague reflection of pain. "You don't look very comfortable." That sounded lame, but she had to slide the bench seat all the way forward to reach the pedals, and the man's knees practically rested against the glove compartment. "I could put the seat back a little." She leaned down to move the lever.

"I'm fine. Besides, if you put it back, you're going to have a tough time driving. Excuse me for saying so, ma'am, but you're not the tall, willowy type."

Matt had often made the same observation. "No, I'm not, am I? But please, don't call me ma'am. My name is Casey. Casey Girard, and this is my son, Jamie." On impulse, she offered her right hand to Chance McCord.

Leaning over, he took her hand in his own.

Awareness of his tall frame and masculine presence sent a zing up her arm, as the rough calluses on his hand brushed against her palm. For a second, he held her fingers in his grip, and when he withdrew, Casey experienced a rush of disappointment and relief. She gulped, as if she'd lost a tiny part of herself. Tamping down the startling reaction, Casey twisted the key in the ignition.

She left the parking space, questions racing through her mind. How had Chance arrived in Jackson? His hat and worn denim jacket showed damp stains from the rain, and he'd asked for a ride. Did that mean he'd been walking when the storm rolled down from the mountains? At the edge of town, Casey put aside her hesitancy. "I know I told Jamie not to be nosy, but...how did you get here?"

Chance glanced down at the boy and winked. Lifting one hand, he stuck out his thumb in a sliding motion. "It's commonly called riding your thumb. Not always a reliable method of transportation, but sometimes, it has to do."

"So, you hitchhiked. All the way from…"

"Colorado."

"Not the safest way to go."

He shrugged. "Didn't have a choice. The engine seized up on my truck. I left it at a junkyard outside of Denver. But don't tell me, you never pick up hitchhikers."

She tossed him a sideways glance. "Usually not. Where I come from hitching is heartily discouraged. My brother and I were forbidden to hitchhike or give a stranger a ride. Parents would've grounded us for the rest of our natural lives if we had. Plus, hitchhiking isn't exactly safe for women."

He met her glance.

Casey caught a glimpse of humor glittering in his deep-blue eyes.

He rubbed the back of his neck. "Can't say I disagree with that. If I ever had a daughter pretty as you, I doubt I'd let her out of the house before she was eighteen."

Casey's face grew warm. Was he flirting? He was brazen all right, but she refused to let his easy banter get to her. Pressing her lips together, she concentrated on downshifting the truck to negotiate a curve. She accomplished the move without a hitch, and the truck traveled down a straight ribbon of highway. She breathed a sigh of relief. "I assure you, Mr. McCord, at eighteen I wasn't much to look at." What her dashing husband had seen in plain, brown-haired Casey continued to mystify her.

"I find that hard to believe."

Casey's heart fluttered. It would be much easier to deal with the Chance McCord who teased and joked and held such a cynical view on life than the gentle and understanding one.

From the corner of her eye, she observed the man who leaned against the passenger door, one arm outstretched along the back of the seat. He was an enigma, for sure—a different breed of man who refused to fit any mold and who marched to the beat of his own drum. She stared at the road ahead. "You're not like your brother, are you?"

Silence chilled the air for a moment.

"And how do you find Kyle?"

His resentment at her remark crept across the truck cab. "Kyle's quiet most of the time, but he seems honest, straight forward, and dependable."

"Not at all like the prodigal, right? I take it you and my kid brother are friends already, although I'm sure he's not a kid anymore."

"He's not." The tall and earnest young man with tousled nut-brown hair who had welcomed them to the North Star a few weeks ago was nothing like his rugged older brother but quiet and handsome in a serious and sensitive way. "Kyle's been kind and helpful to Jamie and me since we arrived."

Jamie looked up from one of his new books. "And he's gonna teach me to ride when he has some free time. Kyle said they got a pony just my size. His name's Buckwheat."

Chance inhaled sharply.

Casey glanced his way. His right hand had tightened into a fist on his knee, but he remained silent, and no visible sign of emotion played across his immobile face. Had she just imagined Jamie's mention of the pony somehow disturbed him?

The highway wound past the rapidly flowing Snake River and took them closer to the Tetons before turning away into the Buffalo Valley. Clouds still hung low over the road and shrouded the mountains until only the tallest of the craggy peaks poked through, wearing a skirt of swirling vapors. Soon, rain fell again. Casey switched on the windshield wipers and focused on driving.

In this short time, she had fallen in love with this wild country and its startling contrasts. With no true foothills on the Wyoming side, the jagged, snow-laced peaks of the Tetons rose straight up out of the mountain valley. More than once in these past weeks, Casey had marveled at them. This early in the summer, the valley had come alive with riotous color—scarlet splashes of Indian Paintbrush, Wyoming's state flower; deep violet-blue Lupine; blood-red wild roses; and the endless clumps of redolent sagebrush. Even in the rain, the sight stirred her soul. How did a man like Chance feel about coming home to such a place?

Forty miles passed, and by the time they turned onto the narrow, paved road that followed the Buffalo Fork, they'd left most of the rain behind them. The sun shot out in a burst of brilliance and beamed down the mountainsides, flooding across the fields and pastures like a path of molten gold.

Jamie leaned forward and pointed out the truck window. "Hey, Mom, look! A rainbow! Isn't it neat? Can we stop and watch it?"

Casey followed the direction of his hand. An arc of iridescent hues curved over the valley. She found a small roadside area where they could watch the colors shimmering in the sky. Pale-melon, bright-turquoise, and goldenrod-yellow all merged in one stunning display that rivaled even the mountain wildflowers. For a long moment, the colors glowed intense and radiant, then slowly faded away into the purple banks of receding clouds. Neither Casey nor Jamie spoke until the special moment passed and the rainbow disappeared. This far-flung country could stir her in so many ways.

"Is it true, Mom?" Jamie asked.

"Is what true?" Casey still stared at the sky.

"Is there really a treasure at the end of the rainbow? And do all your dreams come true there?"

Her heart full of love, Casey gazed at her son. A light of hope shone in his eyes—Matt's eyes. If only she could protect Jamie from further pain in his life. He'd already experienced too much for a child of seven, and she feared making promises. But didn't all children need some magic in their lives? She had to let him believe in the promise of the rainbow's end. "I'm sure there is a treasure, Jamie. I like to think heaven is at the end of the rainbow."

Jamie studied her intently. "Is Dad there?"

A lump rose unbidden in Casey's throat. She hadn't cried for Matt in a long time, but Jamie's pain could still make her tears flow. "Yes," she whispered. "He is."

Jamie settled back in the seat, acting content with this answer.

Casey pulled onto the highway again.

Jamie's eyelids drooped, and he fought off a yawn.

"It's still a way to the ranch," she said. "Why don't

you take a little nap, honey? You were up awfully early this morning."

Too sleepy to argue, Jamie took off his hat and inched closer to the man beside him. "Can I lay my head on you?" He yawned widely.

Chance had not spoken the whole time they'd watched the rainbow.

For a moment, Casey thought he might ignore Jamie's request, but he curved his arm around the boy's small shoulders.

"Sure, partner," he said in a low voice.

The boy promptly nestled his head against Chance's side. In the next minute, Jamie fell asleep.

Only the hum of the engine and the soft swishing sound of the tires on the still-wet pavement broke the silence in the truck cab. Casey didn't try to make conversation but drove along, wondering if a man like Chance McCord could ever believe in rainbows and promises. She bumped onto the dirt two-track that led to the North Star and rattled across the first cattle grate.

"You can let me off here."

Casey jumped and glanced at him, puzzled. "But it's still two miles to the house. It might rain again."

"I've walked farther and in worse weather. The day I left the ranch, I walked down this drive. I know how long it is."

What had made Chance leave? Why had he stayed away so long? The questions spun in her mind and remained, even after he slipped away from Jamie and climbed out of the truck.

Before closing the door, he bent down and peered across the seat at Casey. "Thanks for the lift. I'd appreciate it if you didn't mention this to anyone."

She nodded.

When he'd gathered his gear from the back, he stepped away from the truck and gave the tailgate a smack.

Casey drove on but couldn't help glancing in the rearview mirror. The saddle and duffel bag still sat on the side of the road, and Chance stood beside them. Would he even show up at the North Star? Or would the wanderlust that had once led him from this valley take him away again?

Chapter 3

The main house of the North Star nestled against a backdrop of pine-forested and aspen-dotted hills, an anchor for all the other ranch buildings. To the west stood two immense barns, many corrals, and a long, low bunkhouse. Farther on, past a stand of cottonwoods, lay other outbuildings and the cluster of guest cabins. Casey drove past the homestead to a single cabin behind a towering pine grove.

She loved Billie's sweet, cozy little house. From the moment she'd stepped through the doorway three weeks ago, she'd felt right at home. Warm, knotty pine paneling covered the walls and reflected the late afternoon sunshine pouring through the western windows. Navajo rugs lay scattered about the polished hardwood floor. Simple furniture, comfortable with age, filled the sitting room. Two matching easy chairs faced the small fireplace, their tapestry backs worn smooth where Sam and Billie had spent many an evening reading and talking together. Between them, an end table held a stack of books and a reading lamp. Angled beside the chairs, a monster of an old rust-brown sofa took up the rest of the room.

Casey let herself into the cabin and carried the sleeping Jamie to the bedroom they shared. She gently laid the boy on the small cot set up in the corner, divesting him of the cowboy boots and hat and drawing a red-and-blue patchwork quilt over him. The rain had cooled the cabin, and she didn't want him to catch a chill and get sick again.

In the kitchen, she put away the few groceries purchased in town before going to the bookstore. A box of her favorite English tea, canned fruit, and chocolate chips for cookies went into the pantry cupboard. Closing the door, Casey glanced at the cuckoo clock above the refrigerator. Nearly four. She would let Jamie sleep another half hour, then it was time to head down to the ranch house kitchen to give Billie a hand with serving up supper for Justin and Kyle and the half dozen ranch hands they employed for the summer.

Most of the wranglers were college students working between semesters, and all had exceptionally healthy appetites. Cooking for them was no simple chore, but Billie had been the boss of the kitchen for over forty years and had no intention of retiring. At one time, she'd told Casey, most of the hands lived on the ranch year-round, like herself and Sam. Now, Kyle hired on seasonal help—young strapping men who needed to earn money for college and weren't afraid of hard work. Only two lived at the ranch all year, Roy and Ed. The wranglers were all an amiable bunch, but they certainly did like to eat.

She'd been up at five this morning, shredding potatoes for hash browns. After driving into town and waiting out the storm, Casey considered a nap, but she would just go to bed early tonight. Tomorrow, Justin wanted to show her an old journal that had belonged to one of his ancestors.

An hour later, she stood in the homestead kitchen, whipping up a big pot of mashed potatoes while Billie stirred gravy in a giant, cast iron skillet. A nicely browned roast, surrounded by whole carrots and onions, sat steaming on a platter nearby while Casey's baking powder biscuits turned golden brown in the oven.

"Fellas should be coming in anytime now." Billie added more flour to the gravy. "I do believe they all have inborn clocks that tell them when it's six, noon, and six again."

"They do," Casey agreed. "It's called their stomachs." She'd become fond of the wiry little woman with the cap of steely gray hair and brisk, efficient manner. A mighty steamroller rolled up in a ninety-eight-pound package, Bille handled whatever came up and went right on with her work. They talked together in the steamy, cheerful kitchen, and Casey remembered what Chance had said about Billie being like a second mother. What would she say if she knew he was back?

"How's this, Mom?" Jamie stood aside to view his handiwork.

Casey had assigned him the nightly task of setting out the plates and silverware and to make sure plenty of butter was at both ends of the long sturdy pine table. "Good job, sweetie." Casey covered the potatoes so they'd stay hot. When the men trooped into the kitchen, she would fill two heavy stoneware bowls with fluffy potatoes and, in no time flat, they would be empty. "Come get the glasses." She handed them down from the cupboard just as someone knocked at the door.

"Now, who in tarnation's that?" Billie drew aside a sunflower-patterned curtain from the window above the sink. She stood on tiptoe to see out, then shook her head, pewter bangs brushing her forehead. "Must be some cowboy lookin' for a job. Probably should just send him on down the road, but knowing Kyle, he'll find something for him to do. The boy hates turning anyone away. I'll just point him toward the bunkhouse." Still mumbling under her breath, she opened the door.

Hearing Billie's gasp, Casey almost dropped the glass in her hand. She whirled about, her heart in her throat. Was someone threatening Billie?

"It's the man from the—"

Casey clapped her free hand over Jamie's mouth. "Hush. Remember our secret."

Billie stood stock still in the doorway, her face pale. Her lips moved, but no sound came out.

Chance leaned down and planted a kiss square on Billie's cheek. "Got an extra plate for a hungry cowboy? Always could smell your cooking a mile away." His glance took in Casey where she stood, one hand still gripping Jamie's shoulder.

For a second, the deep-blue eyes searched hers, and she nodded so he would know she'd kept her word.

"Chance McCord," Billie finally sputtered. "It's-it's..." Lost for words, she simply threw her arms around the man's middle and gave him a hard hug.

His returning embrace lifted the tiny woman right off her feet.

"Now, you put me down, you hear? Just because you're built like a bear doesn't give you the right to maul people." Laughing, Billie slapped at the arms that held her so effortlessly.

Seeing Billie's joy, Casey breathed a small sigh of relief for Chance. He'd crossed the first hurdle.

His own laugh ricocheted around the kitchen. "I swear, Billie Murphy, you haven't gotten any older, only a lot feistier." He set her back on her feet and held her at arm's length. "Nope, guess I was wrong. I do see a new wrinkle there." He touched Billie's cheek in a tender, teasing gesture.

Like a bee swatting a bear, Billie knocked his hand away. She stepped aside to let him enter the steamy kitchen.

Chance didn't argue and grabbed his duffel bag from the porch. He dropped the bag beneath the row of hat hooks just inside the door.

"Land sakes, man, do you realize the start you gave me?" Billie drew a shaky hand across her forehead. "Thought you were some old traveling cowboy lookin' for a job."

She pushed him to sit at the long table and stood staring, as if she still couldn't believe he had come home.

Sobering, Chance lifted the cowboy hat from his head and let it drop on his knee. "To be honest, Billie, you weren't too far wrong."

Her smile faded a bit. "You must have come a long way. Did you get it all out of you, Chance? The need to run? Are you truly home now?"

He stared at Billie. "I don't know. I suppose that depends on Justin…and Kyle. Being away this long was no solution, but I had to leave. I had to get away from here."

"I know." She stopped him. "And I understand." She rested her small wrinkled hand tenderly against his rough-and-shadowed cheek.

Chance grasped her hand. "You always did, Billie." His voice sounded husky. "You and Sam."

Anguish filled his words.

At the mention of her late husband's name, Billie sank down beside Chance at the table. She still gripped his hand fiercely. "Sam's gone, Chance. We lost him last winter. There was an acci—"

"I know. I heard from someone in town. And about Justin's being sick. I'm sorry I wasn't here. Are you doing okay?"

Billie wiped away a few tears. "Sure I am. Now you're here, I'm going to do even better. You know how Sam and I felt about you, Chance. The last conversation we had was about you. He was wishing so much that you'd come home." Billie's voice caught.

Casey suddenly felt like an intruder on their conversation. Maybe they should leave the two of them alone. She started to steer Jamie toward the seldom-used dining room down the hall from the kitchen.

"Don't leave, Casey." Billie waved her back into the room. "I want you to meet Chance, Justin's older son."

Casey and Chance pretended they'd never met. Even Jamie kept quiet.

The stomping of boots on the back porch cut the conversation short. In a second, the kitchen filled with laughing, boisterous men. They'd all washed up for supper and dressed in clean jeans and work shirts. Billie Murphy allowed no dirt in her kitchen.

Casey set to dishing up the meal and passing bowls down the long table. The wranglers filled their plates, and even the unexpected cowboy had plenty. Another of Billie's codes—no one left her kitchen hungry. Everyone got busy devouring the food, and the noise sank to a dull roar. Casey slid into her place next to Jamie and noticed two empty spots at the table. Justin and Kyle had not yet come in to supper. Was Justin not feeling well again? In the past week, he'd begun to look so much better. If only he hadn't taken advantage of that and done too much today.

Billie passed a basket of biscuits down the table and sat beside Casey. "I'm worried Justin and Kyle aren't back yet," she whispered. "That man just can't seem to obey doctor's orders. A problem came up with the irrigation ditches. Somebody upriver is using more than their share of water, and our canal is low. Kyle had to investigate, and Justin insisted on going along. Next to Sam, he's the stubbornest man I've ever known."

"He's so used to being active, I'm sure it's hard for him to stay down. I'm sure Kyle won't let him get overtired." Casey smiled and patted Billie's hand.

"I know. Kyle's been a real help to his father through all this, and maybe it's better they're not here tonight." Billie's gaze drifted to the other end of the table.

Chance sat quietly eating like one of the hired hands. The other wranglers accepted him as a new man who had just hired on. The prodigal son hadn't bothered to tell them any different, only giving them his first name.

"I don't know how either of them is going to take this. Five years with no word from someone is a long time."

What could've happened to make Chance stay away so long? Watching him sit at the table and let them treat him like another drifter in need of work put a peculiar ache in Casey's throat. From experience with her own father and brother and Matt, she knew all about men's pride and how they had a hard time dealing with its loss. From the looks of things, Chance had swallowed a lot of pride in just coming home.

After supper, Casey sent Jamie out to play with Mariah, the furry beast of a dog who ruled over the ranch yard.

The men thanked Billie and Casey for the meal and left to finish the few evening chores before retiring to the bunkhouse.

Chance waited until they were gone to rise from the table. He stood slowly.

Across the room, Casey heard the crunch of a bone and saw him wince. He limped to the door and picked up his duffel bag.

Billie's sharp eye caught the movement. She grabbed his arm and forced him to sit back down. "You're hurtin', aren't you? What happened, Chance?"

He tried to grin and shrug it off. "Aw, you know how it is, Billie. Just a little stiff from hitting the highway too long. My bones aren't as young as they used to be."

"Yeah, well I don't think that's all there is to it, and you might as well tell me. I'll get it out of you sooner or later."

He might be reluctant to talk, but Billie was insistent.

She kept a tight hold on his shirtsleeve.

"It's just my fool knee." He rubbed his hand hard over his left knee. "I broke something a while back, and it hasn't knit yet. I just need to stay off it for a day or so, and I'll be okay. Kicks up if I use it too much."

"How did it happen?" Billie persisted. "Rodeo?"

"Not hard to guess, huh? How else would Chance McCord bust himself up?"

Billie propped her hands on her slim hips. "One of these days, you're going to break your neck."

"One of these days, I'm going to quit. As in now, as in I'm all washed up. I haven't rodeoed in almost a year. Not since this happened. I'm all through, Billie." He shrugged in a careless way.

Casey sensed he didn't feel indifference. More like bitter resignation.

"You mean that?" Billie frowned. "Is that the only reason you've come home?"

Casey washed a pan in the sink, but she glanced up to observe the man at the table. Fatigue creased his rugged features. Maybe Billie should just drop the questions for tonight. Chance was exhausted, and did it even matter why he was back?

He got to his feet and headed for the door, this time ignoring Billie's restraining hand. Thumping his hat against his leg, he stared at the floor. "I guess I came back because I've got no place left to go." He jammed the hat down on his head, hoisted the duffel bag over his shoulder, and swung open the door.

A cool evening breeze drifted down from the mountains.

"Your room's still here." Billie took a step toward him. "I could fix it up for you in a jiffy."

"No, thanks, I'll take the bunkhouse 'til I know how my coming back sets with Justin and Kyle. Who knows, I might even leave tomorrow. They might not want me here."

"They'll want you," Billie promised. "You're still Justin's son, and he's never stopped loving you, no matter what happened. You are his firstborn. He had a lot of plans for you."

"Yeah, and we all know what I did to those plans. I think it's a little late to count on me to fulfill any hopes for him now. Leave that to Kyle. I just want a place where I can live and work and draw a paycheck. That's *all* I want out of life anymore. Just a place to be." He stepped onto the porch and picked up his saddle. At a slow, uneven gait, he ambled past the cottonwood grove and toward the bunkhouse.

Shaking her head, Billie watched him go.

Casey turned to stack dirty dishes for loading the dishwasher. The ache in her throat had morphed into a giant lump she needed to swallow.

In Billie's cabin later, Casey built up a small fire to ward off the sharp nip of the mountain night. She'd tucked Jamie into bed, and usually, by now, she and Billie were ready to turn in, but neither one felt inclined to call it a day.

Curled in one of the big easy chairs, Billie stared into the yellow-orange flames crackling around the log in the grate. She wore a man's red plaid robe that engulfed her tiny figure and made her appear older than her seventy years. She said Sam's old robe helped her feel his presence.

But tonight, maybe the unexpected homecoming made Billie pensive. Casey wanted to say something that wasn't prying but might help the older woman talk about what troubled her. Wrapping a fleecy blanket around her flannel pajamas, Casey gave the log a final poke and plopped down in the twin easy chair. She tucked her legs beneath her. Three weeks ago, she and Billie had spent several nights sitting and talking about how losing Sam and Matt had changed their lives. Now, neither of those two men occupied their thoughts.

Billie smiled wistfully, the lines drawing deeper creases at the corners of her eyes. "You don't have to sit up with me, honey. You look mighty tired. Why don't you turn in?"

Casey's eyes grew heavy, but too many questions played in her mind about the oldest McCord son and why he went away. She rested her chin in her cupped hand. "I can't help thinking about Chance, Aunt Billie. You said he's been gone five years, but what I don't understand is, why did he leave in the first place? He just doesn't seem the sort of man who would up and reject his family for no reason. He was very upset that Sam is gone. Much more than you know."

Seeing Billie's quizzical glance, Casey realized what she'd given away. But did it matter now if Billie knew about the meeting in town? "I know this sounds crazy, but Chance and I met even before you introduced us." She explained about the storm, the crowded café, and the ride she'd given him to the ranch's first gate. "Honestly? When he asked me to let him off, I suspected he might turn right around and head back to the highway. I think he wanted to come home but doubted he'd find a welcome sign. Not to be nosy but why does Chance feel that way?"

Billie shook her head and waited a moment. "To understand Chance the man, you have to have known the boy. From the time he was born, he wasn't easy to handle. Nobody could keep a rein on him. Always riding up in the hills and wanting to strike out on his own. Justin had big hopes for him one day taking over the ranch, but Chance had other ideas. All he ever wanted since he was a kid like Jamie was to follow the rodeo circuit. He was always hanging out at the rodeo in town. While his mother was alive, he respected her wishes and stayed home, but Alicia died when Kyle was nine and Chance eighteen. For Chance, that was it. He had no more reason to stay." Billie wrapped her robe closer around her. "He left home just a few months later. By the time he was twenty, he was pretty well-known. By twenty-two, he'd won best all-around cowboy in Cody. Sometimes, he'd come home for a day or two, but mainly to see Sam and grab a little rest between rodeo dates. The rift between Chance and Justin grew wide, and there was never any love lost between the brothers. Kyle grew up with their father's condemnation of Chance ringing in his ears. It's something he's never forgotten."

"What a shame"—Casey shook her head—"for a father and his sons to be so torn apart." Her own family had their issues but no serious rifts. "But it's been a few years since Chance was twenty-two. What happened in between?"

Billie sighed and reached into the drawer of the lamp table beside her chair. She lifted out an envelope and fingered it. "Forgive me for not going on. It's not that I don't think you should know. It's just that the telling is hard, and right now, I'm not feeling up to it. I think I'll just sit here and read for a bit. Why don't you turn in? Five o'clock comes early, you know." She slipped the envelope back into the drawer and picked up her book.

Casey went to bed, but she didn't sleep for a long time. What was in that envelope? Something that had to do with Chance's leaving. Maybe the answer to a lot of questions.

Chapter 4

According to Billie, Justin McCord's thick hair had long ago turned the color of the snow that topped the Tetons. Matched by his neatly trimmed mustache, they were the only clue that hinted at his seventy years. Rangy muscles still hardened his tall, lean body, and not much escaped his sharp silver-blue eyes. He sat across from Casey at the massive mahogany desk in his study and house library, and his face reminded her of a relief map of Wyoming—full of rugged planes and deep furrows, marked here and there by the rise of a hawk-like nose, curved cheekbones, and a wide chiseled brow—truly a Western face.

Justin glanced up. "Something troubling you this morning?" He arched one bushy eyebrow. "Or am I boring you silly with this nonsense of mine?"

"Of course not." Casey shook away her idle musings. "And telling me the legacy of the North Star isn't nonsense." She motioned toward the small brown leather book that lay fragile in Justin's big hands. "I was thinking about how much you must resemble your great-grandfather the way his wife described him." *And how much Chance resembles you.* "It sounds like he was a rugged and independent individual. No wonder she fell in love with him."

"Garett and Martha were married for nearly sixty years." Justin stared down at the journal. "And yes, they were a strong, self-sufficient people. That's the sort it took to settle this wild, untamed territory back then. In the late 1800s, they needed a lot of gumption, not to mention just plain stubbornness, to come here and homestead. The big ranchers said they had the right to control the land. The two sides constantly feuded." With one gnarled finger, he traced down the thin papery page of the journal. "In this passage, Martha expresses very real fear they would be driven off their land. If she hadn't believed things would get better, she might not have stuck it out with Garett."

"Oh, I believe she would have. How could she leave a man whose 'voice sounds like thunder rumbling down the mountains and whose eyes remind me of a clear summer sky'? I think Old Grandma Martha was a true romantic, even if she had to be tough to survive."

Justin chuckled. "So, you were listening, after all. Thought maybe for a minute there I'd put you to sleep."

"Not where history's concerned. It's always been my great love, sometimes to my disadvantage."

"How's that?" Justin leaned back in his swivel chair and studied Casey.

A pleasant camaraderie had sprung up between the two over their shared interest in the journal, and she found it easy to talk. "For one thing, in high school I always passed history exams with flying colors. No one else in class scored as high, and the teacher graded on a curve. My friends were all mad at me. On vacation, I insisted we stop at every historical marker along the way. Matt was patient, but I know how history bored him. Matt loved computers and airplanes. He studied technical journals, and I loved all the old musty history books." Talking about this didn't cause the pain it once did, but other things still did. Things like the memory of cross words spoken in a moment of frustration. Words she could never take back.

"Yet, you were happy together," Justin said.

Casey plucked at a string on her faded jeans. "We were." *Most of the time.* "I loved Matt…so much, and I'm thankful he gave me a beautiful son."

"Marriage can be wonderful…or not so wonderful. Alicia and I had twenty years together, and not a day goes by I'm not thankful for those years. It's just…"

A faraway cloud drifted into his eyes. Who was he thinking about? Not Alicia. Speaking of his wife never evoked the sadness that shadowed his face right now. She motioned to the yellowed pages with the faded script. "Would you like me to read for a while?"

Justin nodded and settled in his chair.

She swiveled the small book to face her and drew it close. The flourishing feminine handwriting of over a hundred years ago was difficult to decipher, but the journal brought alive, as no history book could, the trials facing a young wife in early Wyoming.

"March 5—Garett just came back from the national park to the north. It's called Yellowstone. I don't think I want to go there. He said it's a place where water shoots up out of the ground in great plumes, and brightly colored pools bubble away like so many boiling pots. Folks called it 'Colter's Hell,' after a man named John Colter. No one wanted to believe the sights he described. I can't say I blame folks. If Garett hadn't seen these things himself, I don't think I would believe.

"There is still snow on the ground, and I long for the freedom of summer. If there is anything I've had a

hard time accepting out here, it is the long winters. In southern Illinois, the trees are beginning to bud, and soon Father will turn up the vegetable garden for Mama before he plants the corn and wheat. Sometimes, I wish I was back there again, but how could I have let Garett go without me? He's so tall and strong and handsome, only death could make me leave him now."

"See, I told you." Casey interrupted her reading and glanced up from the journal, expecting to see Justin smiling. She saw something quite different, and a sharp stab of fear stopped her cold.

Was he having another attack? His lips paled, and he stared straight ahead at some point beyond Casey. She followed his stricken gaze and met up with a pair of eyes that spoke of turbulent western skies.

Chance stood just inside the doorway, the curled brim of his cowboy hat clutched in his hands and broad shoulders thrown back in a defensive stance. Tension radiated from every taut muscle in his body and fairly crackled in the room; his jaw twitched as he clenched it.

Casey's heart skipped a few beats. How would Justin accept his elder son's homecoming? Was he ready to forgive? Or would he turn his back on his prodigal son?

Justin rose to his own six-foot-plus height and stepped around his desk. Three feet away from Chance, he stopped, and the two men stood eye to eye.

Casey shrank a little lower in her chair. What if Justin ordered his son out of the house? Facing Justin like this had to cost Chance a ton of pride, and if she heard the old man tell him to leave, she could never quite feel the same about him.

Justin shook his head. "Welcome home, son." He

put out his right hand to Chance. The two men shared a vigorous handshake, and then Justin pulled his son against him in a rough embrace.

Sudden tears stung Casey's eyes, and she rose and slipped unnoticed out of the room. Outside, she stopped on the back porch and swiped at her cheeks. If Matt could see her now, he'd have a good laugh. He'd always called her a real softie who cried at the happy parts in movies.

Leaning against the porch railing, she sighed and gazed out toward the mountains that loomed across the valley. They'd come to represent strength and unity, the sort of unity a family should have. Had Martha McCord found inspiration living so near them? Or had the mountains only made life harder when snowstorms rolled down their rocky slopes?

Maybe a quick stroll out to the corrals would drive away her sudden melancholy. She found Jamie hanging on the fence, watching Kyle work at halter-training a young pinto colt. "Having a good time?" She folded her arms along the top rail and propped her chin on them.

Jamie pushed up the brim of his hat on his forehead. "Yep, I sure am. Kyle's showing me how he breaks the colts. Only he doesn't call it breaking. He gentles them."

"That sounds like Kyle. I don't think he'd ever do anything that wasn't gentle."

Kyle spoke softly to the young horse and taught it to accept a rope and halter.

He was such a contrast to his older brother. Even while facing his father in the library, Chance had worn a hard mask. Since yesterday, Casey had only seen the mask slip when he talked about Sam Murphy. Maybe

Justin's acceptance of his son's return would soften Chance a bit.

"I saw Chance this morning," Jamie informed her. "He said I could call him Chance. Is it okay, Mom?"

"Sure, so long as he doesn't mind. Did you notice if he talked to Kyle at all?" Shame on her for pumping Jamie for information, but she had to know if the two brothers had confronted each other yet.

Jamie frowned and stared at her with his little boy eyes. "They did, Mom, but they sure didn't seem happy to see each other. If Chance has been away so long, how come Kyle isn't glad he's home?"

With her fingers, Casey combed a sweep of pale-blond hair from Jamie's forehead. "I don't know the answer to that. It must be something that happened a long time ago. Something they've never gotten over."

"But I like them both, and I want to be friends with them. Do you think they'll mind?"

"Of course not. Their problem has nothing to do with you, and I'm certain they both like you." In spite of Chance's reservation where it came to his family, he had been friendly enough with Jamie. But was it a good idea for her son to idolize the man? She couldn't be sure but made up her mind not to let the boy make too much of a hero out of Chance.

They talked for a while and watched Kyle work with the yearling.

Finished with the training session, Kyle let the colt loose into an adjoining corral. He joined them at the fence. "I thought you and Dad were reading that journal today." He took off his dusty hat and perched one foot on the lower rail, resting both elbows on his upraised knee. The hat dangled from his long fingers.

His amber-brown gaze, so different from his brother's stormy blue one, rested on Casey.

"Did you give up for the day already?"

"Not quite. Something drew Justin away." She climbed atop the fence to sit and studied Kyle's smooth handsome face. At twenty-five, he still had a beguiling boyish charm about him. Surprising no local rancher's daughter had set her sights on Kyle by now, but then he didn't spend much time away from the North Star except on ranch business. Did he even have a social life?

Kyle glanced away, a grim frown crossing his handsome features. "I suppose you know about the homecoming. I saw Chance heading for the house. How did my dad take seeing my brother?"

She shrugged. "Very well. He was shocked at first, but then incredibly happy. When did you first know Chance was home?"

He showed no surprise at Casey calling his brother by his first name. "Billie told me this morning before anyone came in to breakfast. She wanted me to tell Dad, but I wouldn't. I guess I figured if I ignored Chance, he'd go away again."

Conscious of her son's rapt attention, Casey suggested Jamie pay a visit to Buckwheat, the placid, aging pony kept in a small corral behind the barn. Jamie loved to sit and feed Buckwheat handfuls of sweet hay.

He trotted along now to the pony's pen but with several backwards glances.

She waited until Jamie was out of earshot to speak to Kyle. "I know it's none of my business and you may certainly tell me so, but why are you and your brother so at odds? It's sad that you're all so divided. Families

44

are supposed to stick together and help each other."

Kyle blew out a sigh. "Chance never did a blessed thing for us. He walked in and out of our lives whenever it suited him. He never cared how we felt. If Dad's happy to see him now, that's all fine and good, but no one should expect me to welcome him home." He strode away, slapping his hat against one leg.

Futility pressed down on Casey. Like a chasm a mile wide, the rift between the McCord brothers loomed large. What would it take to bridge that gap?

The question still niggled at Casey when she set out to find Chance later that day.

"You tell that fool of a man he better get in here and eat a decent meal tonight," Billie insisted. "Knowing him, he's been living on beef jerky and soda, and if he thinks he's doing that here, you tell him he's got another think coming."

Chance didn't eat breakfast at the big house this morning, and Billie had fussed the whole day about it.

Casey had no intention of telling Chance any of this but would simply say Billie expected him at dinner tonight. Rehearsing in her mind just what to say, she didn't notice Chance striding out of the barn and promptly collided with him. In the next second, he grasped her shoulders to keep her from sprawling in the dirt and held her tightly before releasing her again.

"Sorry about that." He bent to pick up the tangle of bridles he'd dropped at their feet. "I was checking these over and didn't see you. Are you all right?"

Like twilight slipping over day, his dark blue eyes skimmed over Casey. Her pulse beat hard at how close he stood, and she stepped back. "I'm fine…really." But that wasn't quite true. Her legs were doing a poor job of holding her up, and where his hands had so briefly closed over her cotton blouse, her shoulders tingled…like she'd touched an open light socket

Chance tipped his head to one side, his hat casting a shadow over his face. "Were you looking for someone?"

Casey managed a small smile and nodded. "Actually, I was looking for you."

He lifted his eyebrows. "Were you now? I'm flattered."

She tipped up her chin. "Well, only because Billie sent me. She wants to know if you plan to eat dinner with the rest of us like a civilized person or hide out like a heathen?"

Chance threw back his head and laughed, the sound echoing through the long barn. "And I can imagine those are her exact words."

"Close enough." She refused to let his teasing get to her and folded her arms primly in a determined stance. "So, are you or aren't you? It would be nice to know how many plates to set out."

He observed Casey for a moment, then dropped his gaze to the bridles in his hands. "You can set one for me."

She tried not to hear his low and husky voice. Her heart had just recovered from that moment he'd closed his hands over her shoulders and kept her from landing bottom first in the Wyoming dust. "That'll make Billie happy." She started to go but was drawn back by Jamie's shout.

He tore around the side of the barn, with the huge furry dog galloping at his heels. Skidding to a stop, Jamie dropped to his knees and hugged the mammoth beast about the neck. Like an amiable polar bear, Mariah leaned against Jamie and gave him a lap with her giant tongue.

"I see you two are getting along." Casey scratched behind Mariah's floppy ears. The dog had taken it upon herself to guard Jamie like one of the young calves on the ranch. "Staying out of trouble, I hope."

"Sure, Mom. We were at Buckwheat's corral. How soon can I learn to ride him? I can't wait anymore." His eyes sparkled with barely contained excitement.

"I'm sure as soon as Kyle has time, he'll teach you." Casey gave her son's ear a tweak. "You have to be patient. He's very busy, you know."

"But summer will be gone before we know it. We'll have to go home, and I won't have learned. Why can't somebody else teach me?" Jamie screwed up his mouth.

Her son's fear of that happening was real and important, and she hated to see him disappointed. Coming to Wyoming had done him such a world of good, and she would do anything to keep him from going back to the pale, somber little boy of a few months ago back home.

Giving in to a motherly urge, Casey caught Jamie up for a quick hug, making a pretense of tucking his rumpled T-shirt into his jeans. "You know the men all have their work to do, sweetie. Maybe next week Kyle will have more time. He says they should be all through with the branding by then. We can go see them work again tomorrow."

Just a few days ago, she and Jamie had watched while Kyle and the other wranglers worked at branding, earmarking, and vaccinating the spring calves. Casey had begged off seeing the dehorning process of the older cattle, but it hadn't bothered Jamie, who found the entire procedure of readying the cattle for summer pasture fascinating.

"Don't hug me, Mom." He struggled to get away and kicked at a stone in the dirt. "I get tired of always waiting."

"If your mom doesn't mind, I could teach you to ride Buckwheat."

Casey glanced at Chance. He took off his hat and studied Jamie. His eyes reflected sadness in their depths.

"Could you?" Jamie beamed again. "That would be so neat!" He folded his hands in an imploring gesture. "Can he, Mom? Please? Then I wouldn't have to wait."

She wavered in doubt. Was it a good idea to allow Jamie around Chance that much? The man's drifter ways hardly made him someone to idolize; yet Jamie would do exactly that if he spent much time with Chance.

Chance shifted his dark gaze to hers. "Don't worry. I won't let any of my evil ways rub off. And I won't encourage Jamie to run off and join the rodeo. You can rest easy, Ms. Girard. I'll just teach your boy to ride."

Flustered he could read her doubt so easily, Casey still hesitated. After all, she had a right to be cautious. Jamie was her son. "I didn't mean to imply you would, nor that I don't trust you—"

"But you don't."

"That's not what I was going to say." From the corner of her eye, Casey caught the unhappy frown on her son's face. *Be very careful.* By denying Jamie this opportunity, she could make him idolize Chance even

48

more. "It's just that as Jamie's mother, I'm responsible for his safety."

Chance's jaw hardened. He offered no retort.

But she regretted her remark. "I didn't mean that the way it sounded, like you wouldn't look out for him, but maybe we should just forget the whole thing for now."

"Aw, Mom!" Jamie wailed. "That's not fair. Why can't Chance teach me? I don't understand." He folded his arms and glared at her.

Casey bit her lip. She wasn't used to dealing with the independence Jamie had started to show. Was this normal at his age? Caught between wanting to make her son happy and needing to do the right thing, she debated what to say. A light clicked on in her head. What she needed to do here was trust. She would just have to trust everything would turn out okay.

She met Chance's cloudy blue gaze before resting on Jamie's pleading little face. "Okay. Permission granted. But please, both of you, promise me you'll be careful."

Jamie leaped at Casey and hugged her around the middle. "We will, Mom. Thanks. Thanks so much." Before he heard Casey change her mind, he ran off to tell the pony they would soon be riding partners.

Casey watched him go. Had she done the right thing? Sometimes, parenting was a struggle. She wished Chance understood the life of a single parent and the weight of having to make all the decisions. "Jamie is all I've got." She breathed a wistful sigh. "Letting go even this much is hard."

"I know."

At least he held no grudge for her doubts. She tried

for a lighter tone. "We'll see you at supper. Billie's in the kitchen baking up a mob of pies. I should get back and help her." She'd gotten only a few steps away when Chance spoke.

"Thanks, Casey."

She glanced back. "For what?"

"For trusting me."

****

An hour later, Chance stopped by Buckwheat's corral. He opened the gate and slipped inside, whistling softly.

The shaggy little beast ambled over.

"Hello, old friend." The pony blew on his shirt pocket and nuzzled his hand, searching for the hidden treat. Chance chuckled and offered one of the two sugar lumps he'd pilfered from the coffee room in the bunkhouse. "You haven't forgotten that, have you? Has anyone else snuck you sugar while I've been gone?" Buckwheat shook his head. "Yeah, I'm glad to see you, too. Thanks for not hating me too much." Chance let him lip the second lump of sugar from his hand.

Buckwheat munched, then lifted his brown and white face for a rub.

Chance obliged him, scratching his forehead and finally allowing the pony to rub his shaggy head on his leg. The practice was an old routine and so ingrained in them both that even five years hadn't erased the habit. As a young colt, Buckwheat had been a gift from Justin for Chance's fifth birthday, and Chance was the first one to put a saddle on the pony a few years later. The two had grown up together. "I guess some things never change, do they? How about it? Are you ready to teach another little boy how to ride?"

At his own words, a sudden wave of pain that didn't stem from his broken knee surged through Chance, bringing back memories so clear that to allow them to linger would leave him unable to exist. They still blindsided him at times, when he least expected it, and then he had to banish them to some far corner of his mind. Only today, the memories stayed. Today, he remembered the sound of a child's voice, high-pitched and joyful, mixing with a man's deep-timbred one. The jingle of a pony's bridle and the sweet laughter of a young boy rang in his mind. The pain of remembering seared like a hot poker through the gut, but Chance gave in to it, because today he hadn't the strength to fight. Because sometimes, the loss was still just too hard to accept.

Chapter 5

Casey slipped out the cabin door into the lingering twilight. Evening crept down the slopes of the Tetons. Their long shadows swallowed up the corrals and the barns and other outbuildings of the ranch, as the heat of the early July afternoon dissipated. A bracing coolness greeted her as she crossed Billie's small front porch. She rubbed her arms against the sudden chill. Good thing she'd worn a sweatshirt. Even in the middle of summer, when the sun dropped behind those formidable peaks, the temperature dropped along with it.

After a month at the North Star, she liked to walk out in the early evening to enjoy a few quiet moments. Jamie and Billie were engrossed in a card game, and they barely noticed her leave the cabin. Her son depended on her less and less to fulfill his every need. A sign he was growing up a little? Maybe. But sometimes, she ached to go back to the time when Jamie was a baby and so totally hers...and Matt was still alive.

She stopped under the cottonwoods and watched the last crimson vestige of color melt away above the purple-gray mountains. For a moment, the sun outlined the ridges with fire. Then the falling shadows put the fire out, and only the faintest glimmer remained to light the path to the corrals.

A group of young horses stood close together

inside the fence, and they nickered.

Mariah sat dutifully beside Casey and nuzzled a blunt, wet nose in her hand.

"Taking up guard, are you?" Casey rubbed behind the big dog's floppy ears.

Mariah rewarded her with a swipe of her warm tongue. She whined softly and shifted closer to rest her big head against Casey's leg. Obligingly, Casey kept her hand on the thick neck, sinking her fingers into the furry white ruff. Together, they listened to the breeze whispering in the cottonwoods and the horses nickering low to one another.

Casey leaned one arm on the top fence rail and propped her chin, closing her eyes to draw around her the peacefulness of the approaching night. A sudden loneliness seeped into her soul. On nights like this, she missed the comfort of an arm around her and the way Matt had liked to murmur in her ear, sending delicious shivers down her spine. He'd been an adventurer, one who liked to fly his airplane more than anything else, and he'd sure known how to wrap everyone around his finger, including her.

A sound broke the stillness, and the sweet, quivery song of a harmonica floated on the breeze. The haunting melody fit in with this far-flung land with its rugged mountains, windswept valleys, and wild rivers. Casey sighed and sank into the plaintive music.

All week, the lonesome songs had drifted over the ranch at night. Which one of the men played the harmonica so heartbreakingly? Whoever the musician was, he expressed a thousand pent-up emotions in the music. Tonight, the notes touched a responsive chord in Casey.

The music crept closer, then faded away into the cottonwoods' rustling branches.

Mariah stirred from Casey's side and wagged her tail in a lazy fashion.

Casey guessed who the intruder was before he stepped up to join her at the fence.

"Nice night, isn't it?" Chance lifted his gaze to the mountains. "The kind of night you long for when the snows start piling up and drifting across the range."

The mountains blended now into a velvet sky of deep-blue.

"When do the snows start?" She didn't mind his intrusion but rather welcomed the warmth of his presence.

"We've had them late as June and early as August. The Tetons are rarely without snowcap. They can get snow any month of the year."

Even now, giant patches left from early summer storms stood out ghostly on the jagged slopes.

"Folks like to say we have only two seasons here, July and winter. My mother used to complain that July lasted only two weeks. It won't be long, and there'll be a nip in the air."

The air nipped enough already. Michigan winters were far from mild, but at least, they arrived a little later.

"So, what have you been doing lately, besides helping Billie cook?"

Sometimes, it felt like that's all they did. "We got the cabins ready for the guests who'll arrive next week. Then Justin and I read more of the journal today." She glanced up at Chance.

He leaned one hip against the fence and tipped

back his hat.

His dark hair waved across his forehead and tempted Casey to brush it back, as she would Jamie's. She folded her hands tightly together along the fence rail. "Martha McCord wrote about a great blizzard they had. It must have been a terribly difficult time."

"Those years were all bitter for the cattlemen. The big barons realized they'd have to share the range with the homesteaders and sheepherders. Fencing had come to stay. We still have a lot of open range, but fencing was the beginning of the end for the old longhorn…and the old ways. I imagine Justin is having a field day telling you all his tales of the McCord family."

He joked, but did she sense a deep longing beneath Chance's words? Perhaps he wished he and his father were closer, and they could share the same rapport. "I think he enjoys having someone to share it all with. He has the time, but everyone else is still busy. Even Billie won't sit still long enough to hold a conversation. She's always seeing to Justin's needs as far as eating properly and taking his meds, but what he wants is for someone to have a conversation. Have you spent much time with him since you've been home?"

Pressing his lips together, Chance frowned and turned away. "It's still too strange. It would've been normal if he'd ranted and acted mad as hell. I was used to that kind of thing between us. This unquestioning acceptance has me baffled."

"Maybe he realizes it's foolish to waste time bickering and holding grudges." Too bad she hadn't realized that herself…until too late. "You should just accept his new attitude and go on from there. The same thing might even work with you and Kyle."

At the mention of his brother's name, Chance growled a low sound in his throat.

She'd noticed no sign of reconciliation between the two men. They sat at the same table and passed each other as they went about their work, but they spoke not at all. Casey didn't understand how they could ignore each other so completely.

Leaning his elbows on the fence, Chance hunched his shoulders and stared hard at the dark mountains. "I don't believe anything will ever work for Kyle and me again. We were never close, and too much has happened to hold us apart."

So much she didn't know and couldn't ask, and yet, Casey longed to reach out to Chance. In the past two weeks, she'd learned to trust him completely with Jamie, and the boy had great fun riding Buckwheat every day. If only she could help the man deal with whatever haunted him. In a friendly gesture, she rested a hand lightly on his arm.

His muscles tightened with tension.

"Don't give up on it. I'm sure you and your brother can find a way to reconcile, if you both want it bad enough." Not knowing what had come between the brothers, did she even have the right to say that?

Chance glanced at her hand, then he slid his deep-blue gaze over her.

His eyes reminded her once more of that sky above the Tetons, only this time, they were as dark and velvet as the summer night.

He tipped his head to one side. "Have you always been like this, Casey? Have you always found life so easy?"

His voice sounded just a pitch softer than the

breeze stirring in the cottonwoods. The question brought back unbidden that stormy autumn night nearly three years ago when Matt hadn't come home. She'd called the airport and found out his plane was late, then missing, then reported down in a gale over Lake Michigan. From that moment on, nothing had been easy, but for Jamie's sake, she'd pushed through the dark days. She wanted to tell Chance this, but the right words just wouldn't come out. "No. But you find a way, even when your whole world is turned upside down."

Their eyes met, and he held the gaze for a moment.

She read the need in him to find something that could make his life whole again. His arm relaxed beneath her hand, and the tension flowed from him as from a coiled spring. She drew her hand away.

He stared back out at the mountains. "Tell me about yourself, Casey. Tell me about a freckle-faced, barefoot kid."

She'd told him once about being raised on a farm in Michigan but lifted her chin in defiance now. "I did not have freckles nor did we go barefoot. My mother would have rather died. My parents own a dairy farm, and so, I was raised around cows. My brother and I used to show them at the fair every summer."

"Did you now? I guess living on a ranch isn't unfamiliar territory. I can just imagine you in long pigtails and faded overalls. I'll bet you were pretty cute."

She heard admiration in his tone but objected to his description. "Well, we weren't *that* hayseed, but about the only time my mom got us into anything but jeans was on Sunday."

"Just you and your brother?"

"Yep. We had a pretty good life, and sometimes, I miss the farm. Getting up in the morning and hearing the rooster crow, smelling warm fresh milk, collecting eggs, and hearing the flap of sheets on the clothesline. The town where Jamie and I live isn't exactly urban, but it's different from the farm. There are days I wish I could go back to that time again."

"Do you visit?"

"Of course. My brother and his wife help run the business now. My folks still live there, but my dad's had some health issues lately. Jamie and I go back on holidays. When my husband…died, Mom and Dad wanted me to move home for a while."

Chance shifted his weight and leaned into the fence more. "You didn't think that was a good idea?"

Casey stared out into the darkness. "They had plenty of room, but I had to put my life back together. I couldn't do it living with them. They mean well, but they'd have made my decisions for me…taken care of me. I didn't need that. I needed to stand on my own…for my sake and Jamie's."

"I hear you," he empathized. "What made you decide to come to Wyoming this summer?"

She hadn't thought about it. She'd just packed up Jamie and left. "A couple of things, I guess. Matt's parents died when he was young. Sam and Billie kept in touch all the time. When I heard about Sam, I knew how lonely she must be. And I felt good about getting away to someplace new and different."

Chance surveyed the ranch yard and the fences that stretched away into what seemed like forever. "I know that feeling. At one time, getting away from here was the only thing in my mind."

"You mean when you were eighteen and wanted to join the rodeo?"

He left one elbow on the top rail and faced her. "Billie's been talking, right? I s'pose she told you the whole sad story."

"Part of it. She said you always wanted to rodeo."

"That's true, and for a while, rodeo is what I did. Hard. Rode every bucking bronc that came my way and got thrown from the best. But those days are over. I should've realized that before a blown-out knee did it for me."

What about the chapter of his life that Billie would not talk about? What had happened between the time when, at twenty-two, he'd been on top of the rodeo world and the day five years ago when he'd turned his back on his family and the North Star? "At least you're home now. It's never too late to start over. Justin is more than willing, and maybe if you'd meet Kyle halfway—"

"So, we're back to that again." Chance lifted one hand and ran the tip of his finger down her cheek. "I think, lady, you are relentless."

Casey let down her guard a little, and his touch sent a ripple of awareness across her shoulders. "Just determined." She was determined right now he wouldn't know how his touch affected her, and how her heart suddenly beat like sixteen jackhammers.

"But a very pretty determined." He brushed his hand, rough and raspy from ranch work, against her hair, then lifted the strands and let them slip over his worn fingers.

The touch was so gentle, Casey's breath caught in

her throat.

"The color…kind of reminds me of a cougar I once saw. She looked soft and tawny, but she had a fighting streak. Do you, Casey? Would you fight me if I kissed you?"

The unexpected question obliterated every sensible thought from her head. Her eyes fluttered upward to see if he really meant it.

He really did. With one hand, he took off his hat and with the other slowly slid his fingers around the back of her head and drew her close.

Through lowered lashes, Casey watched his dark head lower, and then the fleeting brush of his lips against her own sent a rush of warmth surging in her veins. His lips were firm and warm, a sweet first taste. But the kiss quickly became something more, something that tasted of fire…and danger…and…

For balance, Casey pressed her hand to Chance's broad chest. Beneath her fingers, his heart tripped in double-time. That she could stir him this much, a guy who'd no doubt kissed more than his share of girls along the way, startled her. For an infinite moment, any semblance of clear thinking flew away on the cool Wyoming breeze, and an incredible sense of coming home filled her heart.

Chance drew back, but Casey still leaned into his warm strength. What was with her legs? Like two quivery rubber bands, they threatened at any second to collapse. Darned if she didn't feel like a teenager on her first date.

With his thumb, he traced a path along her jaw and across her lips, where the imprint of his kiss still lingered. "That was nice," he murmured. "I enjoyed it thoroughly. Did you?"

She wouldn't lie, even if a twinge of guilt lurked in her head, as if she had betrayed someone. Of the two dates she'd gone on last fall, only one had ended with a kiss. That kiss had only served to prove she wasn't yet ready for any sort of relationship. She'd told her sister-in-law Cindy to stop trying to set her up. But this cowboy's low and sexy voice knocked her equilibrium off-kilter. "I'm a little out of practice. I'm...sure you can tell." Her voice wavered.

He shifted closer. "Not too out of practice, but I'd be glad to show you again just how it's done."

Casey was ready this time. She stood on tiptoe, met the kiss, and curled her fingers into his shirtfront. The heat of his skin beneath the fabric warmed her. He shifted, leaned her against the fence, and put his arms around her, drawing her into his embrace. Mesmerized, she sank into his tall solid frame, feeling him from head to toe. Somewhere, in the back of her mind, good sense wanted to prevail. Yet she couldn't hear it speaking too clearly...or didn't want to. She only knew Chance and the call of a nightbird. Chance and the rustle of the cottonwoods. Chance and the steady thrumming of her heartbeat in her ears.

Chance stopped the kiss. Groaning softly, he buried his face in Casey's hair before setting her away.

The cool night air rushed between them and sent a chill racing down Casey's arms. She shivered.

"You better go in," he said. "C'mon. I'll walk you to Billie's cabin."

They didn't touch while on the pine-needle strewn path. Once at the cabin, Casey's teeth chattered with nerves. "Will you...have a lesson with Jamie tomorrow? I'll…come down to the corral…and watch."

Chance crammed his hat on and tilted the brim down low over his face. He put space between them. "Sure. Just bring him down after lunch." His hat hid whatever emotion glowed in his midnight-blue eyes.

Casey nodded and started for the door. She stopped and glanced back. He was already striding down the path, a funny hitch to his gait. She sighed and touched her lips. Had the kisses meant anything? Or were they only a moment to pass the time?

Inside the cabin, Jamie and Billie were already fast asleep. Casey tucked the quilt snugly around her son and kissed his forehead before putting on her flannel pajamas and crawling into bed. For a long time, she lay awake, listening, waiting to hear the sweet sad song of that harmonica, but no haunting melody drifted on the mountain breeze.

****

Chance stretched his long body on the narrow bunk without bothering to undress. Clasping his hands behind his head, he stared at the ceiling and watched the play of moonlight and shadows that crept through the window. The moonlight had played on Casey's hair that way and turned it to a color somewhere between the gold of the aspen in the fall and the rich tawny brown of a mountain cat's fur. The strands felt like silk slipping over his fingers and her skin like satin. Her eyes reminded him of two pools of tranquil water that, without her knowing it, invited him in to drown himself.

Like a fool, he'd let himself get drawn and had flirted at the edge of those gray pools, forgetting for a few bittersweet moments he'd taken a vow never to feel this way again. He needed the comfort Casey could offer, but he surely didn't want any more pain. Pain was all he'd get if he let this thing go any further. Casey wasn't the kind of woman he could just have a fling with. She would get into his head and claim his heart. He couldn't deal with that.

And besides, what did a broken-down cowboy have to offer someone like her? Nothing serious could ever exist between him and a lady with class. That she had let him kiss her was simply spur of the moment overriding her good judgment. Probably she'd always wanted to kiss a cowboy. Well, she'd gotten her wish. Now he had to figure out how not to let it happen again.

He struggled to sort that out long after the other men had turned in for the night and their snores filled the long, low bunkhouse. He'd slept in plenty of bunkhouses on nameless ranches and was used to the enforced, often crude, lack of privacy. The noise of a dozen or so men settling down for the night didn't bother him. At least, this bunkhouse was peaceful. Some were hothouses of bad tempers and repressed feelings ready to boil over at the first wrong word. But his own feelings kept him awake tonight, as thoughts of Casey knotted his stomach in a tight ball. The torment prevented him from sleeping, until long after the moonlight deserted the cottonwood outside the window to chase its shadow across the Teton mountain range.

Chapter 6

The main house of the North Star Ranch gave the impression of having stood in the valley forever. The McCord family home for over a hundred years, the house and the twin blue spruce that flanked the front porch welcomed visitors. As Chance entered the house the next day, the history of those McCord pioneers weighed heavy on his shoulders.

Inside the homestead, mahogany and leather furniture of the last-forever sort spoke of masculine tastes. A native stone fireplace dominated the living room, and a wide picture window faced the mountains, affording a spectacular view of the Tetons in the distance. An impressive house, but one that hadn't seen the loving touch of a woman's hand in many years, not since Alicia McCord died. Her influence had faded, except for the muted murals of western scenes that graced the walls. An artist in her own right, Alicia had painted them during her life here. The murals, as well as her two sons, were her donations to the North Star legacy. Seeing the paintings now added another burden to the coming home decision. Losing his mother had been the first great sorrow in his life. If he stopped to think about it, Chance could feel the loss like it was yesterday.

He paused before knocking on the door to his father's study. How many times as a kid had his mother sent him here? Too many to count. Alicia didn't quite know how to handle the stubborn, single-minded child who was her firstborn son, though she loved him fiercely and never stopped efforts to set him on the right path. Afraid he would end up permanently injuring himself, she often sent him to his father for counsel. But whatever words Justin spoke pretty much went in one ear and out the other. Chance could never be the man his father wanted, so why try? He often berated himself for causing his mother so much grief. She'd wanted what was best for him and because of her, he hadn't left the North Star sooner. When she'd passed, leaving had been easy.

If only coming home could be the same.

Steadying himself with a deep breath, Chance removed his hat and rapped lightly on the heavy wooden door. A few seconds passed before he heard a muffled, "Come in."

Justin leaned back in his desk chair, facing toward the tall windows of the study, hands folded over his chest. In years past, Chance would have expected to see his father bent over the desk, poring over the thick ledgers that recorded all the business of the ranch. When he wasn't working the cows, Justin spent hours crunching numbers, struggling to keep the ranch going in the lean years. At least, that's what Sam told Chance when he complained that his father didn't listen. As a teenager, Chance hadn't understood the stress that drove his father to work countless hours. Now he saw the toll those hard years had taken. How much had his own behavior affected his father?

Justin didn't turn around. "Just set them down on the desk. I'll take them later."

Chance hesitated in the doorway. "Pardon?"

Justin swiveled in his chair.

Chance glimpsed the fatigue that furrowed the older man's face.

"Chance! I thought you were Billie with those confounded pills she's always making me take. Seems every time I turn around, she's there with another handful."

"She's just trying to help." Chance stepped into the imposing room. "I'm sorry. Did I wake you? I can come back—"

"Nonsense. Sit down." Justin motioned toward the easy chair. "I was just sitting here thinking. Seems like some days that's about all I can do."

Still uncomfortable in his father's presence, Chance took the chair across from the desk. Resting his elbows on his knees, he let his hat dangle from his fingers while he mulled around in his mind what he had come here to say.

"So, how are things going so far?" Justin asked. "Is Kyle giving you enough to do?"

"He is. Just riding the fences and handling some repairs. Doing whatever needs doing."

"I'm glad you two are working things out. I always hoped my sons would run this place someday. Nothing would make me happier." Justin sat a little higher in his chair and waited.

Chance just nodded. He didn't want to talk about Kyle. As far as he was concerned, nothing had been settled between them…and maybe never would be. Justin would have to accept that, but the last thing he wanted was to cause his father more grief. Chance didn't reply.

Justin swiveled back toward the windows. His gaze traveled to the mountains that lay in the distance. "I remember how your mother and I used to go riding in the mountains. She loved going up first thing in the spring, as soon as the trails were clear of snow. She wanted to hear the waterfalls. How she loved waterfalls. Seems a lifetime ago now."

To me, too. Before Justin's reminiscing could get to him, Chance cleared his throat. "I'd like to talk to you about something." He didn't think Justin had heard or, like so many times before, just wasn't paying attention. Chance nearly got up and walked out.

Then suddenly Justin faced him.

The silver-blue eyes pierced him, as they so often had in the past.

"So talk."

Unable to speak while his father scrutinized him, Chance stood and crossed the room to stare out the windows. "I have an idea for bringing in some extra cash here at the ranch. While in Colorado, I worked with an outfit that trained the mustangs they round up on the range. They sell them to the national park and forest services to use when the rangers go into the backcountry. Mustangs are sure-footed, strong, and not afraid, and if trained properly, they'll take you anywhere you ask them to go. Some even make good trail horses for the guest ranches."

"And you think you know how to train them now?" Justin shifted in the chair and leaned forward. "What about the initial cash layout? You get them for free?"

"Of course not, but they do sell them cheap. I'm not asking for money. I've got some set aside. Not much, but enough to get started. Whatever pay I draw working here, I'll put back into the business. I don't need much to live on. What I do need is the space, some pasture, a place to keep and train them. They will have to be quarantined at first."

Justin rubbed his chin for a moment. "Seems you ought to be asking Kyle about your plan. In case you haven't noticed, he's in charge now."

"I've noticed, but I'm asking you." Chance summoned the nerve to make the request. At one time, he'd sworn never to ask his father for any quarter again. But if he wanted to stay on here, he needed something of his own, that didn't belong to Kyle or Justin.

He stood at the windows, staring hard at the green pastures of the North Star that spread across the valley. By inheritance they were his, too, but he'd never once in his life felt a part of them. Maybe with the horses he could connect. Maybe in time…

"I hear Morly Hanson's got a few mustangs at the Double Diamond. He bought them after the last roundup in the Checkerboard. You might want to talk to him about it and maybe work out something to help train his wild ones, too."

Relief sifted through Chance and eased the tension that had thrummed in the room. He met Justin's steady silver-blue gaze. "I'll do that. Will there be a problem, you think?"

"With Kyle?" Justin waved away that concern. "I'll handle him."

"I won't need much space."

"We're not using the far north pasture. You can have it."

Chance nodded. "Thank you." Two words he'd not said to his father in a long time.

Justin held up one gnarled hand. "Not necessary. You're my son, too, Chance. Even if you didn't always want to acknowledge that."

Gripping his hat, Chance headed for the door. Before he left, he glanced at the place where a small portrait had once sat atop Justin's bookcase—a portrait of three people, two now gone. How long had the spot been empty? "Where is the picture? Why isn't it here?" Had removing the photo wiped out the memory?

Justin took a moment to reply. "Because seeing it every day became just too painful, son."

Chapter 7

The turquoise sky went on forever on the sweet clear day. The Tetons poked their craggy peaks into the brilliant blue with no clouds that might bring rain to the valley. A perfect day for riding, except Casey didn't know how she'd gotten talked into doing the riding. Yesterday, after his riding lesson, Jamie had told her about going to look at horses with Chance. Casey raised her eyebrows.

Chance held up one hand. "Now don't get all huffy." He watched Jamie lift the saddle from Buckwheat's back. "The boy's doing very well, and I thought we'd take a ride over to the Hanson's place tomorrow. They have the next spread, the Double Diamond. I talked to Justin about my training mustangs, and he said Morly's got a couple young colts that need training. Thought I'd see what we can work out."

"Me and Chance are gonna check them out," Jamie added.

Jamie riding outside the safety of the corral? Casey wasn't ready for this. She folded her arms in what Matt used to call her "lecture" pose. "It sounds like you've already told Jamie he can go. How am I supposed to tell him he can't?"

Chance lifted one shoulder. "You're not, but if you like, you're more than welcome to come along. A few hours out in the fresh air might do you some good. You can't spend all your time in the kitchen and Justin's study. You need to blow the dust out of your hair."

Dusty hair indeed! A few nights ago, he'd compared her hair to the soft tawny fur of a cougar. Yet, as was the case whenever Chance teased her, she couldn't stay angry. Seeing her son's eager little face, Casey sighed. "What time do we leave?" Before coming to the North Star, the last time she was on a horse was in college when she went with friends to a riding stable. The young wrangler Roy gave her a few riding lessons her first weeks at the ranch, but after a day of sitting on a horse, she would have a sore rear end.

Billie got wind of the ride. "You'll need a hat and a decent pair of boots," she insisted.

Now, Casey stood in the big house's front hall. She wore a jute cowboy hat, maybe as old as Billie herself, and a pair of red boots resurrected from some closet. "I think I'm going to get warm." She picked at the long-sleeve cotton shirt Billie also insisted she wear. The sleeves clung to her arms. "How far is it to the Hanson's place? I'm not sure why we can't just drive."

"Good four or five miles across the valley." Justin leaned against the wall and stroked his mustache. "Long enough for you to get one nasty burn. The sun can get pretty intense, and you and the boy aren't used to it."

That was true on Casey's part, although Jamie, despite generously applied sunscreen, had tanned brown as a little nut in the last few weeks. Hard to believe he was the same child she'd brought here in June. She could barely keep up with him; he was so full of energy and enthusiasm.

She glanced at her watch. "I better get going. I'm supposed to meet the guys at the barn as of right now. Thanks for the hat and boots." She gave one last rueful tug at the hat, tilting it at a rakish angle. She tossed Justin and Billie the same kind of grin. "Why don't you two think of something interesting to do this afternoon? Take a drive. Go into town. Leave some sandwiches for the wranglers, and they'll be fine. I should be back in time to help with supper." She peeked over her shoulder, wondering if any electricity existed between the two, though romance seemed the furthest thing from Billie's mind. Maybe because for her, romance had died with Sam.

Billie ignored Casey's comments and Justin's hopeful looks. "Who wants to go into town?" she grumbled. "Too darn many tourists this time of year. Or any time for that matter. I can't stand those crowds, and heaven knows Justin shouldn't be overdoing himself. Tagging after Kyle again the other night to that ranch owner's meeting was bad enough. How on earth a person expects to get well traipsing all over creation like a—"

"I have not been traipsing around." Justin sighed. "I just need to get my strength back. I can't do that lying around like some old dishrag. I declare, woman, you are enough to drive a man crazy."

Casey left them to their bickering. Maybe they preferred that sort of relationship.

Behind the barn, Jamie sat astride Buckwheat. He waved to Casey with one hand, while clutching the reins with the other. "Hiya, Mom. How do I look?"

"Like a real cowboy. Just pay attention to what you're doing." She glanced about. Where in the heck was Chance? Did he really go off and leave Jamie alone like this? The boy wasn't ready to handle the pony entirely on his own.

Kyle walked out of the barn.

Casey waved. "Have you seen Chance? Jamie and I are supposed to ride with him to the Double Diamond."

A frown crossed Kyle's face, and he took off his hat, running his fingers through sweat-dampened hair. With a jerk of his head, he motioned toward one of the pastures. "Here he comes now. Guess he went to get your mounts."

Tipping her hat, Casey shaded her eyes against the sun. On the path to the barn, Chance moved in a rolling stride that today bore only a trace of a limp. Behind him followed two horses of remarkable coloring. The taller horse, a smoky gray, had a healthy scattering of white spots sprinkled across his entire body. The smaller, more delicate coppery roan had a rump as white as snow on the mountain. Small red spots flecked the white background and frosted the rest of her sleek body. Her long, silky mane and tail gave the mare a sweet feminine appearance next to the rangy, big-boned gray.

"Gee, Mom. I think you're gonna ride the red one. She sure is pretty." Jamie stared at the two animals Chance led up to the fence.

They were both beautiful horses, and Casey's mood lifted. Maybe riding wouldn't be so bad after all.

"Are they Appaloosas?" Jamie leaned forward in his pony saddle to study the two horses.

"Sure are." Chance looped the bridle reins over the middle rail of the fence and ducked under them to come around to the left side of the mare. "I raised these two from foals some years ago, but Kyle took care of them.

Did a fine job of it, too."

Casey waited to see if Kyle accepted the small olive branch Chance offered.

Kyle glared hard at Chance. "I wanted to sell them, but Dad wouldn't let me. He insisted they were your favorite horses and when you came home, he wanted them here waiting. Sam took care of them. I had more important things to do."

Chance clenched his jaw, and anger clouded his face.

She couldn't blame him. He'd made the effort to meet his brother halfway. Why couldn't Kyle go the other half? But the brothers' problem was none of her business and interfering might make matters worse.

Kyle stalked off.

Chance glowered.

This wasn't a good way to start out the ride, but Casey refused to let the brothers' bad mood ruin the whole day. "What's her name?" She slid a hand over the mare's silky neck and glanced up at Chance. "She is a beauty."

He focused his attention on saddling the mare. "This is Dakota. She's a gentle lady and will suit you perfectly."

Dakota turned and rubbed her velvety nose against Casey's hand. Casey crooned soft, nonsensical words and combed her fingers through the white-frosted forelock that fell between Dakota's ears.

"She's eating that up, you know." Chance spoke low and stepped closer. "See her ears, the way they're pricked forward? She's responding to your voice. I think you could spoil Dakota rotten in no time flat."

Casey cleared her throat. "Who's spoiling? I'm just

making friends. I wouldn't want Dakota to decide she didn't like me halfway to the Double Diamond and leave me in the dirt."

Chance chuckled. "You can be sure if you do fall off, I'll be there to catch you."

He spoke the words lightly, but after the kisses they'd shared, Casey couldn't take them that way. The memory of how his lips, warm and seductive, had played over hers dwelled fresh in her mind. "Trust me. I will try very hard not to fall off," she murmured.

Chance lifted another saddle from the fence and hoisted it over the gray horse's back. Beneath the faded-brown plaid of his shirt, long, lean muscles rippled.

With his collar open at the throat against the day's heat, revealing a vee of tanned chest and snug jeans riding low on his hips, he exuded a raw masculinity that sent Casey's unwitting pulse into overdrive. She fought to tamp down her reaction.

He caught her watching and winked.

Casey's heart raced and gave her a jolt. She swallowed hard, and, for the umpteenth time, she relived those moments by the corral. Had Chance done the same?

He turned away and checked the cinch on the gelding's saddle.

Jamie rode his pony closer and asked a million questions about where they were going, how far, and would they see other horses? Amazing the man didn't mind the boy's insatiable curiosity and even encouraged Jamie to ask questions. His patience just never ran out. What a shame Chance hadn't settled down long enough to marry and have kids of his own.

He might have made a wonderful father.

"Ready to go?"

Casey hadn't realized he was standing so close and jumped at the slight touch of his hand.

"Ready as I'll ever be." If only Dakota proved as gentle as Chance promised.

Holding his hands together, he motioned for Casey to step into them and gave her a boost into the saddle. He tucked the reins into her hands and made sure she was comfortable before turning to the horse he called Smoky. He had a little difficulty getting himself astride but once in the saddle, Chance appeared very much at home, like a figure straight out of the Old West.

She gathered the reins and urged Dakota to follow him. Her backside protested immediately at the inhumane treatment. Tonight, she would soak for an hour in a tub of hot water and bath salts.

For nearly an hour, they rode along the fencing that enclosed the grazing land of the North Star. A peaceful ride, though not a silent one. The sound of creaking saddle leather and jangling bridles accompanied them, joined now and then by Mariah's woofs as she chased after a zigzagging jackrabbit. In the background drifted the lowing of the black Angus cattle that roamed over the range.

The valley itself teemed with the clicking of summer insects and the exuberant trilling of songbirds, but through it all, an even larger voice drifted and spoke in a subtle roar, touching Casey's soul and filling her with all its wild and rugged elements. Not long after arriving at the North Star, she'd learned a truth. *In Wyoming, you could hear the land.*

Chance reined Smoky toward the riverbank. He

motioned for Casey and Jamie to follow and pulled up beneath a whispering cottonwood. "Let's take a break here."

Glad for a brief respite from the sun, Casey lifted her hat and dabbed at her forehead. She watched the river flow lazily past.

"This is the Buffalo Fork of the Snake River. It's running slow today." Chance leaned forward on the saddle horn. "The fork is the dividing line between the North Star and the Double Diamond. If we wait a couple minutes, we might see some of Morly's mustangs here."

Casey and Jamie followed Chance's lead and dismounted, leading Dakota and Buckwheat to drink at the river. Hooves and boots crunched on the loose rocks.

While the horses drank, Chance offered Casey and Jamie one of two canteens of water.

Jamie imitated the way Chance drank deeply and then wiped his mouth with the back of his hand. "Where are the horses?"

Chance nodded toward the other side of the river. "I think, if you're real quiet, you'll see them soon."

Casey leaned against Dakota and watched. The man had a sixth sense about horses. In a moment, the small band of mustangs made their way from behind a scrubby hill down to the river. Several had the markings of Appaloosas. Even though Casey hadn't been around horses much, this group endeared themselves the minute she spotted them. She especially loved the three mares with leggy foals at their sides.

Jamie shaded his eyes against the sun reflecting off the river. "I wish we could get closer. I'd like to pet the babies."

"Afraid that wouldn't be a good idea." Chance rested his big hand on Jamie's small shoulder. "The mares are protective of their little ones. But listen up, Jamie-boy, and I'll tell you a bit about the Appaloosa, and we'll see how much you remember later."

Chance squatted down beside Jamie so he was eye-level with the boy.

Jamie leaned against the man, and the two stared across the river at the horses.

An easy friendship had developed between the man and the boy, and a wistful longing tugged at Casey's heart. A part of her still harbored resentment that Matt wasn't talking to their son, but the discontent faded a bit today. Listening to their voices rise and fall, one so deep and full and the other young and eager, lifted her spirits.

"The Appaloosa takes its name from the Palouse River in Idaho," Chance told Jamie. "The Nez Perce tribe bred them for many years, but the breed wasn't discovered by the white man until the explorers, Lewis and Clark, traveled west. Buffalo Bill Cody used the Appaloosa in his Wild West show many years later, and the breed became famous. Their roots trace back to Spain, but the Nez Perce kept the breed alive."

Jamie slid one arm around Chance's shoulder and hung on every word the man spoke. "Are they still here...the Nez Perce?"

Chance sighed and gave a slight nod. "Many were killed in surprise attacks by the army. That was a dark chapter in the history of the West, but the tribe is still recognized today, and the Appaloosa survived. It's sometimes called the Nez Perce horse. See that mare?"

He pointed out a dark horse with white spots scattered over her body. "That's a snowflake Appaloosa. The white ones with black spots are leopards. My horse, Smoky, is a white-blanket and your mom's horse, Dakota, is a frost."

"How come the babies don't have spots?"

"They will as they grow, but their markings might be different from either of their parents. That's what makes them such an interesting breed." Chance stood and rubbed at his knee. He took off his hat to brush an arm across his brow.

"I guess you like them, huh?" Jamie tilted his head back and gazed up at Chance. Frank admiration glowed in the boy's blue eyes. "You know a lot about them, and you know somethin' else? I'm gonna be just like you when I grow up."

Chance's face darkened. He settled his hat on his head again and jerked the brim down. "We best get going. I told Morly to expect us about two."

The sun poured like warm honey across the valley, but a sudden chill hung in the air. Chance changed quickly from friendly and informative to cool and remote. He didn't talk much on the rest of the ride, and to Casey's relief, they arrived at the Hanson's ranch house a short time later.

The Double Diamond, like the North Star, was a working ranch, as well as a dude ranch. Guests had started arriving here a few weeks ago, and the place bustled with activity.

Morly Hanson, a red-faced, husky man with a blustery voice, took time out from his paying guests to welcome Chance, Casey, and Jamie. "Good to see you, man!" Morly slapped Chance on the back and bellowed toward the rambling brick house. "Marianne, Jeannie, come on out and see who's here!"

Two women appeared on the porch. Both were tall and slim with shiny dark hair and flawless oval faces.

Casey could not decide if they were mother and daughter or sisters.

They hurried out to greet Chance. The one who appeared slightly older hugged him. "Chance, oh my gosh, it's so good to see you. We heard you were back in the valley. You know how word travels in these parts." She turned to Casey. "Hello. Welcome to the Double Diamond. If you haven't guessed, I'm Jeannie, Morly's wife. You must be Billie's niece who came out for a visit. I'm sorry we haven't been over to say hello, but the work just doubles once the guests arrive. Is this your boy?"

Jamie stepped up and offered his right hand. "I'm Jamie, and this is my mom, Casey."

Everyone laughed at his solemn introduction.

Jeannie offered her slim hand to the boy and then to Casey in warm greeting. Brushing back her short, feathery-styled hair, she put out an arm and drew the younger woman near. "This is my baby, Marianne. Though I guess she's not a baby any longer. Can you believe it, Chance? Mari turned twenty-one last month, and she's fresh out of the university with her degree in elementary ed."

Marianne blushed a little.

She was a pretty young woman with long umber hair that swung nearly to her waist and fell forward in a soft curtain when she nodded.

Marianne glanced toward Chance, a light shining in her hazel eyes. Then she went up to him. Sliding her hands into the back pockets of her snug jeans, she shook back her curtain of hair and glanced up. "We missed you at my party, but it's good to have you back, Chance. The valley wasn't the same without you. Every time we got a new horse, Pop would say, 'Wish Chance could see him.' Now you can. Welcome home."

He smiled in that slow, easy way Casey had come to know, letting his gaze drift over the girl's trim feminine figure.

"I think your mom's right. You're not the skinny kid I remember. I'm surprised Morly hasn't married you off yet. What's wrong with the local male population? Are they blind?"

A soft flush of apricot stained Marianne's cheeks, and she shook her head. "No, just mostly already married or spoken for."

Except for two. Did Marianne already have her sights set on Chance? Perhaps she had for a long time, despite the age difference.

"Anyway, it's good to have you back in the valley again." Jeannie waved toward the house. "How about we all go inside for something cool to drink?"

"I'd rather stay here and look at the horses." Jamie inched over toward Chance. "I'm not so thirsty."

Casey chewed her bottom lip. "All right. Just don't wander off by yourself."

"I'll watch him," Chance promised. "And we'll be along in a few minutes. I could use a glass of Jeannie's lemonade myself."

Morly hauled Chance over to a corral where several horses nosed at a broken-up bale of hay.

Casey joined Jeannie at the house. In the shade of the Hanson's front porch, she plucked the jute hat from her head and dabbed her shirtsleeve across her sticky forehead. This had to be the hottest day they'd had this summer, and Chance would pick it to go for a ride.

"Here, why don't you sit and rest for a bit?" Jeannie straightened the cushions on the porch swing.

Casey didn't argue and sank onto the cushions. She stretched her legs out in front of her and winced at the rawness creeping through all her muscles.

Jeannie disappeared into the house but returned shortly with a pitcher of frosty lemonade and several glasses. She filled one glass and set it on a little table beside the redwood swing. "You look about all done in. I take it you don't ride much."

"Haven't ridden in years. I probably wouldn't have come along today, but Jamie had his heart set on it. I didn't want to disappoint him. Chance has been teaching him to ride, and my son practically hero-worships him."

"Jamie would have been perfectly safe with Chance. He's always been super careful around horses."

Casey took a long swallow of the lemonade, letting the tangy sweetness soothe her dry throat. "I know, and it's not that I don't trust Chance. It's just…"

Jeannie smiled. "I understand. I was very protective of Marianne when she was small. Sometimes I still am. She's our only child."

"She's a lovely young woman." Casey tipped the cool glass against her temple. She glanced to where Marianne had taken Jamie inside a small corral to pet a young colt whose mama didn't seem to mind.

Marianne held the gangly-legged youngster around the neck while the boy stroked the colt's shiny withers and giggled.

"I'll bet she's good with children and will make a wonderful teacher."

Jeannie settled in a porch chair opposite Casey. "Marianne has applied for a few different positions, but I wish she'd stay local and live on the ranch. She helps me with the guests and the cabins and loves working with the horses, but I know she needs to get out on her own. It's just hard to see them grow up and away."

Casey wouldn't face that for a few years, but her own parents had clung when she'd wanted to move away. "Is there anyone special in her life?" The words came out of the blue, and would Jeannie even admit if her daughter truly carried a torch for Chance?

"There is." Her gaze rested on her long-haired daughter. "But she'd die of embarrassment if I ever told anyone. She thinks I don't know, but Morly and I have both known for a long time. It's just too bad some men are so blind."

A twinge of jealousy pricked at Casey. How ridiculous. After all, she and Chance had only kissed a few times. No sense making it into more than that. She sipped at her lemonade and banished the silly emotion.

Jeannie's gaze narrowed, and she studied Casey for a moment. "So, tell me about yourself, Casey. You're from Michigan, is that right?"

Glad to talk about something other than Chance and Marianne, Casey told Jeannie about her life in a small lakeside town, her job at the library, and her love of history.

"Justin told Morly just last week about how you're helping him with this book he wants to write. How's it coming?"

"Mostly we've sorted through old photographs, letters, and a journal he has, figuring out how we can incorporate them into the book. He wants to include some local history. He talked about visiting the historic trail at Menor's Ferry today, but Chance and Jamie had other plans for me." Rubbing at her sore legs, Casey grimaced. "Somehow, I think riding is what I'll remember the most about my trip to Wyoming."

"Well, you can't come to the cowboy state without riding," Jeannie said. "That's just a given. Besides, we have so much to see here and the best way is on horseback."

She chatted with Jeannie for a bit about the beauty of the Grand Tetons and the valley of Jackson Hole.

"We've lived here all our lives, but we don't take the grandeur of the mountains for granted," Jeannie said. "When we married, we decided to stay in the valley. There've been a lot of struggles and hardships, but I've never changed my mind."

"I can be thankful for that." Morly's voice boomed out as he stepped up on the porch and helped himself to a glass of lemonade. "How would I be able to run this place if I didn't have my sweetie?" He grinned and winked at Casey.

No doubt Morly, a burly, exuberant man, acted gentle as a kitten around his wife. She liked the Hansons for the way they had welcomed Chance without any questions.

"Nice boy you got there, Casey."

Morly used her name as if he'd always known her.

"We always hoped for Mari to have a brother, but it didn't happen. Now we're looking forward to grandchildren. That is, if she'd get busy and find herself a husband."

Marianne came up on the porch. "Pop!" She flushed and looped the curtain of dark hair behind her ears. "I just got out of college, and you make me sound like I'm an old maid or something."

"I hardly think you have to worry about that." Behind her, Chance leaned his tall frame against the porch railing. "But if you like, you can come over to our place. Kyle's hired on a whole string of handsome wranglers who'd probably give their eyeteeth to meet you."

A shadow crossed Marianne's face.

Casey glanced between the two of them. Apparently, Chance had no idea the young woman had a crush on him. If he did, he would not be so cruel and tease her this way.

Jeannie shook her finger at the men. "That's enough, you two. Just because I married so young doesn't mean Mari has to. She should live a little first."

"Ah yes, my child bride." Morly leaned down and gave his wife a resounding smack of a kiss on her cheek. "I raised her, you know. Had fun teaching her, too."

Jeannie gave him an elbow nudge. "I'm not sure who you think did the teaching, but I kind of think it was me."

They all had a good laugh at the rancher's woebegone expression before the talk turned to horses, and he and Chance discussed training the mustangs.

Nearly an hour passed before Marianne nodded toward the sky. "Are we supposed to have a storm? Looks like it's getting a little dark over the mountains."

To Casey's surprise, the jewel-like turquoise color

had given way to deep violet-blue, and a thin mist of clouds topped the jagged peaks. Great, just what they needed, to get caught in a storm on the ride home to the ranch.

"Guess we better head back." Chance handed his empty glass to Jeannie and shoved himself away from the railing. He winced.

Casey kept silent. The Hansons might be good friends, but he would not want them to know an injury forced him back to the North Star.

The three Hansons accompanied them to where Chance left their horses.

"Hope you can get home before the storm hits." Morly watched the rapidly darkening sky. "Maybe you ought to just wait it out here."

"We'll take the shortcut along Silver Canyon." Chance helped Jamie mount up. "It shouldn't take that long. Storm might even blow past us by then." He turned to Casey.

She stepped into the saddle by herself. She didn't want Chance giving her any special attention in front of Marianne but also needed to prove she didn't need help. She might be ten years older than Marianne, but the younger woman's capability around horses made Casey feel lacking.

Jeannie approached Casey and extended a hand. "I'm glad we got to meet today. You tell Justin and Billie we all should get together soon for Sunday dinner. We've got a couple of wranglers who can look after the guests for a few hours."

"I'll do that." Casey gave Jeannie's hand a returning squeeze. "See you soon, and you, too, Marianne." She nodded to the Hanson's daughter and received only a brief smile in return. As she turned Dakota to follow Chance and Jamie, Casey debated if Marianne was jealous of her riding with Chance today. The last thing she wanted to do was get between them, if something really wasn't going on. For the sake of her own heart, maybe she best keep her distance from Chance.

Chapter 8

Casey appreciated Dakota's sure-footedness, as they followed a narrow trail into the high country on the way home. Along the rim of a steep granite canyon, whitebark aspen grew ghostlike, their shiny, round leaves shimmering gold-green in the pungent air. The storm appeared to have skirted the valley, and the sun filtered in thin beams through the tree canopy. The brushy trail wound through stands of pine and hardwood and crossed a tumbling creek that flowed cold and clear straight out of the mountains. Riding single file limited conversation, but Casey didn't mind. The peacefulness of the mountain forest settled around her.

She found it less stressful on her leg muscles if she relaxed instead of holding herself so rigid, and she moved languidly with the mare's easy pace. She'd gotten the idea from Chance and envied the natural way he sat on the big gray, as if his tall body became one with Smoky. No doubt the grace evolved from years of riding. A person didn't learn in one afternoon.

They left the wooded canyon behind and began the descent into the valley. With a sudden rush, the wind picked up. The soughing sound through the pine trees gave Casey a chill.

Mariah, padding silently alongside the horses, stopped in the middle of the trail and panted.

Smoky turned antsy, twitching his ears back and forth and snorting. He sidestepped along the narrow trail, refusing to go on.

Chance kept the gelding under control, with his voice low and soothing and hands firm on the reins. He swiveled in the saddle, looked around, and muttered.

Casey followed Chance's line of vision. They had reason to worry. The storm had not drifted away, and they would not beat it home. Purple clouds rolled in over the canyon, obliterating the dancing sunbeams. The trail fell under shadow, and a deep rumble vibrated down the mountains. Casey leaned forward and patted Dakota's neck to soothe the mare.

"Sorry, but I think we're about to get doused." Chance reined Smoky around. "It's moving in fast."

A sulfur-yellow flash of lightning snapped above the tallest pine tree, followed by another growl of thunder. The rumble rolled past them and echoed to the canyon wall and back.

All three horses danced skittishly.

Chance drew Smoky up alongside Jamie. "Heads up, partner." He leaned down and steadied the pony before lifting the boy from his saddle. "You ride up here with me for now." He perched Jamie in front of him and handed the pony's reins to Casey, then curved one arm around Jamie's middle to keep him from falling off. "The ranch house isn't that far, but I don't want us caught in open country in a storm. We'll have to hit some cover."

Cover sounded like a good idea, but where would they find shelter? The dense stands of aspen and pine might offer some protection from the rain, but they were also good targets for lightning. They'd passed by a place where brittle white skeletons—remnants of a lightning fire—stood as mute testament.

"What're we gonna do?" Jamie tipped his head up at Chance.

"We're gonna keep you and your mom from getting wet, so just hang on, son. We've got to move pronto. You okay, Casey?"

Her own "yes" sounded a bit uncertain even to her own ears, but she gripped the pony's reins tightly.

Chance settled Jamie against him in the saddle and nudged Smoky into an easy lope.

Casey let Dakota follow suit, and hugged her knees to the mare's sides, praying she would stay on...and lightning wouldn't strike them. Bringing up the rear, the pony trotted mightily to keep up.

Casey urged Dakota on, and the mare followed Chance into a small clearing just as the first raindrops kicked up splotches of dirt from the ground. A cabin in the early stages of decay provided a sorry, yet welcome, sight. At least, it would offer some protection from the mountain-bred storm.

As the weather front rushed in over the high peaks, a fierce gust of wind blew away the last of the day's heat and shrouded everything in a heavy blue mist.

Chance vaulted from his saddle, even before Smoky slid to a stop. "Get inside," he barked and thrust Jamie into Casey's arms. "I'll put the horses in the lean-to." He snatched the reins from her and tugged the wild-eyed animals into the lean-to off to the side of the cabin.

The wind whipped around them. Casey held onto her hat, and, with her other arm, she clung to Jamie and struck out toward the cabin door. She made it to the slanting stoop just as the fast-moving clouds ripped open. A torrent of icy rain streamed straight down in a solid wall, cascading off the brim of her hat and plastering her shirt against her back.

The door refused to budge at first, but a swift kick changed the stubborn wood's mind. An odor of dank mustiness greeted her. Inside the cabin, two small square windows let in only a minimum of light, and Casey let her eyes adjust to the darkness before she took another step. She glanced around at the rough wooden planks on the floor and the primitive furnishings. At least, the log walls seemed sturdy enough.

"It sure stinks in here!" Jamie struggled to get down.

"I suppose it's been closed up for a long time." Casey let him go and lifted his cowboy hat, shaking off the clinging water. They were both soaked, and the dampness of the cabin, while sheltering them from the torrent outside, chilled her to the bone. Teeth chattering, Casey drew Jamie's small wet body close. "Let's find a place to sit. If we huddle together, maybe we can stay warm."

"But where's Chance? Isn't he—?"

The door burst open, and Chance charged inside. Sheets of rain blew in behind him, splattering across the cabin floor. A gust of high wind tore like a banshee down the mountains, accompanied by a massive rumble of thunder that shook the cabin walls. "Whew! What a mess." Chance slammed the door shut and sluiced rivers of water from his arms. He swept off his hat and shook it, stamping his boots while puddles formed around him on the floor.

"Did you leave Mariah out there?" Jamie ran to peer out one grimy window. "Won't she get wet and scared?"

"Don't worry, son, Mariah will be fine. She's bred for bad weather. She's a mountain dog. But she's in the lean-to. She'll help keep the horses from getting spooked."

Standing in the shadowy light of the small cabin, Chance's tall figure filled the room. He'd tossed his hat on a hook by the door, and his hair glistened like silver-tipped black satin. His plaid shirt and worn jeans clung, outlining hard muscles, long legs, and a wide chest. What did her own wet shirt display where it lay plastered against her? She plucked the sodden material away from her skin.

The action didn't escape Chance's attention. "You did get drenched. How about Jamie?"

"Nope, I'm okay." The boy peered out the window. "Are we gonna get stranded here?"

"Only 'til the storm's over." Chance steered them both farther into the room. "It'll be gone as quickly as it blew up."

"Oh darn, but I wanna be stranded."

Obviously to Jamie, this was just one big adventure. "You do? Why?" Casey frowned. Getting stranded up here in wet clothes was the last thing she wanted to happen. Especially with Chance so close. His presence charged the cabin with its own electricity. Perhaps as dangerous as the lightning outside.

Jamie turned from the window and glanced around the room. "This reminds me of a movie I watched with Grandpa. Some people got stranded in a cabin all winter up in the mountains. They couldn't get to town and had to shoot a deer to eat and spend Christmas there and cut down their own tree. Wouldn't that be neat, Mom?"

"Yeah, really neat," Casey murmured. Unable to share her son's enthusiasm, she wrapped her arms around herself and paced back and forth.

"Why don't you sit over here on this bench?" Chance pointed to a narrow wooden seat against one wall. "I'll get a fire going."

An old potbelly wood stove occupied one corner. A chimney pipe still jutted from the top and poked through the back wall, probably rusted from disuse. Casey wheeled about. "But couldn't the whole place go up in smoke?"

He grinned and shook his head. "It won't. Come on, Ms. Girard, give me a hand."

"I don't know." Casey hung back, even though goose bumps prickled her freezing arms. A crazy vision of the cabin turning into a blazing inferno filled her head. "When's the last time anyone even used this place?"

Chance didn't answer but strode over to the stove and squatted in front of a box of firewood with long stick matches sitting on top. He opened the door of the stove and brushed the remnants of a previous fire into a pile. Then he built a fresh fire, laying kindling and small pieces of wood in a careful pyramid inside. Crumpling a sheet of old newspaper from a stack near the wood box, he stuffed it beneath the pyramid and struck a match to it all. The paper quickly disintegrated, but the dry tinder caught the flames. Soon, blessed heat poured from the stove's belly.

"Come over here and get warm." Chance straightened and brushed dusty hands across his damp jeans. His gaze traveled over Casey where she stood in the middle of the room, hugging herself. "The stove's not going to blow up, Casey." He spoke a trifle softer. "Please, come over here and warm yourself."

The lure of the fire's heat proved too tempting. Casey tugged Jamie along and sidled over to the stove. Shivering, she held out her hands toward the radiating warmth.

Chance dragged the wooden bench close to the stove, and the three of them huddled together, falling silent to the storm's tirade. Rain pelted the cabin, while the wind buffeted the trees. Their shadows played through the windows and danced against the log walls.

When the lightning flared, Casey saw the cabin's spare furnishings. A crude wooden table occupied one corner and held an old camp stove. A narrow bunk built into the opposite corner looked hard, and she shuddered to think of anyone spending much time in the Spartan, almost primitive room.

She stole a glance at Chance. His eyes appeared darker than ever in the half-light of the cabin. Weariness etched his face, and his hair lay rumpled where he'd run his fingers through it. The lines carved around the corners of his eyes crinkled even deeper than usual. Absently, he rubbed his knee, and a grimace crossed his features. No doubt, the dash to the lean-to and then the cabin had been wrenching. She had been such a baby about building the fire and let him crouch by the stove and do it himself. She wouldn't blame him for thinking her a silly woman. Marianne would have been much more capable in such a situation.

He kept his gaze fixed on a growing wet spot on the floor. "Guess I need to do some patching up around here. Place is getting a little rundown."

A little? What would he consider a lot? "How long has this cabin been here?" *Keep him talking. It'll drown out the storm.* Warmth crept through her, and she ran her hands through her hair to loosen the wet strands.

Chance watched her a moment, then glanced away again. "Since Justin was just a boy. Back then, a ranch hand would stay up here most of the summer, keeping an eye on the stock left to graze open range. Even when I was a kid, they used this line shack, but Kyle tells me he wants to experiment with keeping the cattle closer to home to protect them from predators. The cabin isn't used much anymore, unless someone comes up here to fish or hunt for a few days. With Sam gone and Justin ill, I expect it's been a while since anybody's come here." He stared at the heat rising from the stove.

Haunted shadows lurked in his eyes. Maybe he remembered the times he'd come up here with Sam. It must hurt to recall those days.

A snap of burning wood drew his attention, and he stared down at the silent boy squeezed between them.

Jamie had fallen asleep against Casey's shoulder. She shifted a bit so his head rested in her lap and smoothed her hand over his small puckered brow, brushing back pale blond hair.

"Poor little partner, all tuckered out." Chance laid a big hand on the boy's arm. "Do you think he's still cold?" He didn't wait for an answer but went to the bunk and stripped a dark wool blanket from its skinny mattress. He gave the blanket several hard shakes and held it by the stove before wrapping it around both Casey and Jamie.

He crouched in front of her, folding the rough wool

fabric clumsily around her shoulders. "There. That should warm you up. I s'pose it smells a little musty, but it'll do in a pinch. It's my fault you two got wet. I'm sorry about that." He took longer than necessary to fix the blanket around Casey, but he didn't meet her gaze. Putting his hands on his knees, he pushed himself to his feet and sat down heavily on the bench.

Casey heard the now-familiar crunch of bone.

He winced.

This time she didn't have to worry about discomfiting him in front of anyone. "I know it's none of my business, but maybe you should still be taking it easy. Knee injuries take a long time to heal."

He shrugged off her concern. "It's the arthritis kicking up in the damp weather. Doc told me to expect it, and that it's just something I'll have to deal with."

"And does riding help?" Did she have the right to say this? Why did she even care about his problems? He'd be out of her life by end of summer, and then none of this would matter. She rubbed her arms beneath the blanket. *I can't let his issues become mine.* Except, she already had.

"Now, Casey-honey," he chided, "don't get your dander up. I appreciate your concern, but it's not worth your worry."

"So, does that mean you don't think you're worth the worry?" She was getting herself in deep here, but she hated he was so down on himself.

He sobered and leveled his gaze on her. "I'm not sure I am."

"I think you're wrong." Casey plunged ahead. He might not like her opinion, but she was giving it anyway.

His jaw tensed, and he faced away on the bench. "Then you tell me who has worried about me in the last five years. My father? My brother? They have managed just fine. If I left tomorrow, then they'd get along again."

His words tore at Casey. "Do you honestly believe that? If they've gotten along, it's because they had to. Sometimes, we do that—get along—because life gives us no other choice. But maybe if you'd all open up a little, you could give one another what you need."

"I don't need anything." He rose and limped to the window.

Casey folded her share of the blanket under Jamie's head and left him sleeping on the bench. She joined Chance at the window and stared out at the gray sheets of rain slanting across the clearing. "You say you don't need anything. Not even the regard of the people who care about you? They do care, you know. You father, your brother, Billie. Your absence was hard on them."

He held onto the silence for a moment, then turned and touched her hair, twining some of it around his fingers. "Do you care, Casey? Does it matter to you what a man like me thinks and feels?"

Just this simple touch made her weak at the knees, but Casey couldn't let him know yet how much she had learned to care about him. She wasn't ready to take that risk. "It matters to all of us, even to Kyle, though he's too stubborn to admit it."

"But I'm not talking about any of them." His voice dropped a notch lower. "I'm talking about you, Casey. And me. And what I feel for you. It's a hell of a lot more than I've felt for one human being in a long while." He lifted a hand to cup her chin and tip her face.

In that moment, Casey knew he meant to kiss her, and kissing her was exactly what she wanted him to do. His lips touched hers with a familiar ease, as if he'd been kissing her for a long time. The windblown scent of the mountain rain clung to Chance, and Casey tasted him until her head filled with a dizzying sensation. Within her stirred needs and desires she had buried with Matt, feelings she thought never to have again. Against all manner of common sense, she leaned into this very different man's embrace.

He closed his arms around her, and for a time, his heart beating against her kept pace with the relentless drumming of the rain on the cabin roof. His mouth played over hers with an urgency that matched her own and begged her to respond.

She gladly did. The storm had closed them off from the outside world, and Casey sank into one where only the two of them existed. She reached up and entwined her arms around his neck. Falling in love with Chance would be easy. Maybe she was already halfway there. But to what end? They were so different and had known such different lives. How would it ever work? Loving a man whose own heart was so closed off could only lead to pain. And yet…and yet…

He stopped kissing her and leaned away, putting space between them "Look at me."

She fluttered her eyes open.

He touched her face and stroked her chin with his thumb. "This is crazy, isn't it? To think there can be anything between us. A beat-up cowboy and a Midwestern librarian. Kind of an odd match."

Maybe, but the man was a darn good kisser. She

would let him kiss her again, but the hesitations that had held her back from seeking any new relationship flooded her head. Those old feelings for Matt were still alive, as well as the guilt. She hadn't dealt with any of that, and until she did…

Chance waited for an answer.

Casey didn't have the one she knew he wanted to hear. "I'm sorry." She drew her hands away. "This is all so sudden, and I…I don't know if I'm ready yet. We're so different, and I'm still—"

"It's okay. I understand." He dropped his embrace "Maybe we are just too different."

Her heart thumped a painful rhythm. "It's not you, Chance. There're just too many things I need to settle in my own head."

He nodded. "You don't have to explain. At least, you're honest. That's more than some women would be." With that, he walked to the door and plucked his hat from the hook. "I'm going out to check the horses. The storm should let up soon. I'll call you when it's time to go."

Fierce regret rippled through her. "Chance, I—"

He held up a hand. "Save it, Casey. There's nothing I need to hear right now, so let's forget all this." He jammed his hat on his head and strode out the door.

The sound of the door slamming woke Jamie. He sat up and rubbed at his still drowsy eyes. "Did Chance leave us here?"

Casey went to sit beside him. "Of course not. He's just outside with the horses. The storm's lifting, and pretty soon, we'll be in Aunt Billie's house. We'll have some nice hot chocolate and a piece of that applesauce cake I made yesterday. Doesn't that sound good?"

Jamie nodded and stretched. "Can Chance have some, too? I bet he's hungry."

"Yes, I'm sure he is." Casey ruffled Jamie's hair. She wasn't ready or able to fill Chance's hunger. No matter how much she might love him, something still haunted him, and until she figured out what, she couldn't fall any deeper.

****

In the lean-to, Chance talked to the horses while the storm blew itself out. The last time he'd been up to the line shack, he'd come with nothing but a sleeping bag, his horse, and a few scant cans of food. He'd stayed until a late spring snowstorm roared down out of the Tetons with subzero ferocity and snow lay thick outside the cabin door.

Sam and Justin had braved seven-foot drifts to come up and force him to return with them. Left to himself, he would've just stayed and quietly froze to death when the wood ran out. Freezing would have been a sight easier than learning to live with a broken heart.

Chapter 9

The following Sunday, Casey agreed to attend church service in the valley. She and Jamie hadn't done that in a while, and she would have begged off this morning. But she'd promised Billie, and Jamie was excited. Justin turned seventy-one today, and after church, they would come back to the big house for dinner. She ran the brush through her hair one more time and picked up her small handbag from the bed.

The sandals she'd bought this past week in town clicked on the cabin's hardwood floor. She checked her reflection in the mirror behind the bedroom door. The yellow-flowered sundress with a full, flirty skirt and matching scarf was also new—the first outfit she'd bought in nearly three years. Splurging on something she didn't need had been fun. She straightened the scarf over her shoulders and applied peach lipstick before joining Jamie and Billie on the porch. She needed to hurry, or they'd be late.

Jamie played on the steps with the toy cars he'd brought from home.

Relieved he'd obeyed her warning not to get dirty, she glanced around. "Who's driving?"

Billie rolled her eyes. "Justin insists he can, but Kyle said he'd come along today. It will do the boy good to get away from the ranch for a while."

A twinge of disappointment pricked at Casey.

Chance probably wasn't joining them. Since that day a week ago, when they'd taken shelter in the cabin, she'd barely spoken to him. He'd kept to himself, coming in only at mealtimes and sometimes not even then. Billie had expressed some worry, and Casey hadn't told her about what happened on that ride besides the storm. She simply couldn't talk about it.

Standing on the breezy porch, Billie patted her hair in place. "I sure wish Chance would come with us, but it's always been hard for him to be part of the family. Even as a child, come Sunday morning, he'd disappear. He'd saddle up and take off before breakfast, and there was no finding him. After a while, poor Alicia gave up. I thought maybe her getting sick might change Chance, but it didn't. Guess maybe he was just meant to be a loner, not needing anybody, or wanting anybody to need him."

"I'm not sure that's true." Casey often glimpsed the haunted shadows in Chance's stormy blue eyes. "I think he wants to be a part of life here at the North Star. Maybe he just doesn't know how."

Billie fussed with her sweater. "Well, until he figures it out, he's not going to be a happy man. Truth is, he's been closed up inside himself for so long he doesn't know how to let his family care about him. Then again, maybe he'd rather stay that way."

Casey shook her head at the remark, but there wasn't time to comment.

The SUV Justin drove drew up in front of the cabin but with Kyle at the wheel.

Justin stepped out and tipped his dark felt hat. "Good morning, ladies and young man. You're all looking very fine this morning." He smiled at Casey, but his gaze rested on the older woman standing beside her.

Dressed in smart teal-green tailored pants and a cream-colored blouse with a sweater draped over her shoulders, Billie looked different from her usual jeans and shirt attire. She wore her hair in a fluff of soft gray curls and appeared less wiry, more petite, and feminine. On Sundays, the men of the North Star fended for themselves at breakfast, leaving Billie free to pamper herself a bit.

Casey was pretty sure Justin noticed. A twinkle of delight danced in his silver-blue eyes.

"Now don't start with your flattering nonsense." Billie bristled and reached for Jamie's hand. "I promised you a big fancy birthday dinner today, and you'll get it. You don't need to butter me up."

"Who's buttering?" Justin grumbled. "I just hope by fancy dinner you mean a round of roast beef and mashed potatoes and gravy and not none of those leafy vegetables you've been making me eat. It's a disgrace when a cattleman can't even eat his own beef."

The strict diet Justin's doctor had ordered after the heart attack kept the old cowboy aggravated. Justin hated the way he had to eat and how adamantly Billie made him stick to the plan. The diet provided a constant source of harassment between the two.

Billie harrumphed and waved them all toward the vehicle. "Let's get a move on, shall we? You know how I hate being late for church."

Kyle came around the vehicle and flashed Casey a rueful grin. "Let's hope church calms them down." He opened the car back door.

Before Jamie climbed into the vehicle, he fixed

both the older adults with a pointed stare. "My mom says it's not nice to fight. You probably shouldn't right before church."

Billie glared at Justin, her brown eyes flashing fire.

"The boy's right." Justin relented first. "How about we call a truce for at least an hour?"

Billie gave him the once-over. "I'll behave if you will."

The two broke into laughter.

Justin wrapped his left arm around Billie's narrow shoulders and gave her a hug.

Casey and Kyle both sighed in relief. Maybe there would be peace...for a while anyway.

During the service, the preacher talked about the story of the prodigal son, who left his father's house to travel afar, squandered his life, and then came home when he had no place else to go. The man's brother resented the fact their father welcomed the estranged son with open arms.

Casey contemplated the story that was so much like the McCord's. At the café that first day in Jackson, Chance had even called himself the prodigal son of the North Star. Would the McCord men ever reconcile their differences? Justin had welcomed Chance home, but Kyle still held resentment. Chance himself did not feel he belonged. But why? What else lay in their past that kept the brothers so divided?

Jamie stuck an elbow in Casey's ribs. "Hey, Mom. Stand up."

Shaking herself from the errant thoughts, Casey rose to join in singing a final hymn.

Outside the church, Jeannie greeted them and hugged Casey. "Heard you got a good dousing that day you stopped by. I hope nobody is worse for wear."

"We're just fine." Casey welcomed the hug that was like an old friend's. "Chance felt bad we didn't wait out the storm at your place, but Jamie and I are pretty tough." They had to be tough to survive the past few years. "How's life at the Double Diamond?"

"Hectic! It's a good year for the dude ranch, but I think Marianne and I are about ready for a break."

Casey glanced to where Marianne and Kyle talked. The young woman's long dark hair was plaited in one thick braid and fell over her shoulder. Her golden skin glowed in contrast against the white eyelet dress she wore. She was tall but still had to tip her head back to look up at Kyle. An unusual animation lit up Marianne's face. Were they talking about Chance?

"How about you take that break today and come on over for Justin's birthday dinner?" Billie broke in. "He's being ornery these days, and it'll do him good to visit with Morly. I'm sure they've got plenty of catching up to do."

Jeannie nodded. They settled on a time and went off to their vehicles for the long drive back.

Later that day, after everyone had eaten their fill of tender roast beef and rich chocolate cake, Casey shooed them out on the front porch to enjoy the mountain breeze. When they all settled, she stood in the doorway and glanced around at the people who were starting to feel like family. Justin sat beside Billie in the redwood glider, his mouth curved in a grin. Jeannie and Morly shared the porch swing, his hefty arm encircling his wife's shoulders in an affectionate embrace. In the corner of the porch, Kyle tipped back on a three-legged stool, as he balanced against the porch railing, his hands busy whittling at some hapless piece of wood. Casey sighed. Sunday afternoons in Michigan were much like this. *Not so different from back home.*

Jamie leaned against Chance on the steps and played with a harmonica Chance had given him. "How does it work? Do you just blow into it?" He held the little instrument up and peered through the holes.

Chance drew his own harmonica from his shirt pocket. "Nope. You put your mouth right on it. Watch." He held it to his mouth, set his lips around the metal, and coaxed out a soft short tune. "Keep your bottom lip relaxed but sealed on it. Then start with holes one and two. Now you try."

Casey watched him help Jamie position his mouth on the harmonica, while Chance did the same with his. A sudden memory of how persuasive his lips had felt on hers just a few days ago sent a little thrill buzzing along her nerve endings. She pushed away from the door jamb. "Let's have some sun tea. Marianne, could you help me?" She motioned for the girl to follow her.

When she carried a tray with glasses and a large pitcher to the porch, Casey poured the tea while Marianne passed the tall glasses around. The younger woman had changed to a slim denim skirt and red scoop-neck T-shirt, and her dark braid fell becomingly over the bright knit material. A tiny twinge of jealousy pricked at Casey accompanied by sympathy for the girl. Chance had joined them for dinner but paid only polite attention to Marianne, barely speaking to her at the table and totally ignoring her now while he and Jamie talked. But the girl didn't act upset.

She nudged Casey. "I was surprised to see Chance at dinner. As I remember, he never much cared for family gatherings of any kind. Of course, today is Justin's birthday."

"Jamie insisted he eat with us. I guess Chance couldn't say no. My son can be very persuasive, and he thinks a lot of Chance. He's a real hero to Jamie." She still wasn't sure she wanted Jamie idolizing a man like Chance, but that horse had already left the barn.

"Maybe a little boy like Jamie is just what Chance needs." Marianne handed Casey two glasses of iced tea. "Why don't you take these over there and join them? I'll finish pouring for everyone else."

Casey accepted the iced tea and went to the steps where Chance and Jamie sat. Lowering herself to the empty space next to Jamie, she handed one of the glasses to Chance. "Have something cool to drink. Jamie, you can share some of mine."

Chance grasped the glass, his fingers brushing Casey's. "Thanks." He took a long swallow of the tea and then winked. "That hit the spot."

For a moment, she flashed back to the cabin again and the way his fingers had touched her face, rough and callused yet gentle and tender. The memory sent a tickle up her arms, and her cheeks grew warm.

His gaze drifted over her for a few seconds, lingering on her legs.

Casey brought her knees up and smoothed her dress down over them.

Clearing his throat, he balanced the half-empty glass on one upraised knee and glanced down at Jamie. "I was just telling your son about Hank, a barrel man who taught me how to play this." He motioned to the harmonica. "Hank was a good guy. He kept the bull riders safe and saved my ornery hide more than once from a deranged bronc. If it wasn't for Hank, I might not be here at all."

"I guess we should all be glad for Hank then." Casey lightened the mood between them. If only they could forget about what happened in the cabin and just be friends. But did she want to forget? The kiss and the embrace they had shared were branded indelibly in her mind…and on her lips. She wouldn't ever forget.

"I think I'd like to be a bull rider," Jamie said. "Is that the most dangerous?"

"The most," Chance murmured, his gaze fastened again on Casey. "That's where the cowboys need the barrel man to distract the bull's attention while they run for safety. A quick-acting barrel man has saved many a downed bull rider."

"Did you ride bulls?" Jamie asked.

Chance shifted his gaze from Casey and stared at the glass in his hand. "Once. That was enough. I pretty much stuck with riding broncs after that."

Jamie flipped the harmonica over in his hand. He glanced at Casey. "Guess maybe it would worry you if I rode bulls, huh, Mom?"

The funny lopsided grin on Jamie's boyish face touched Casey's heart. "Just a bit." She offered him a swallow of her iced tea.

He gulped thirstily before dashing off to play a game of tag with Mariah. The two romped together across the ranch yard.

"Jamie has been begging for a dog. I should think about getting him one back home. What breed is Mariah?" *Good way to change the subject, Casey.*

Chance finished his iced tea and leaned back on the steps. "Great Pyrenees, a true mountain dog. Both her parents were champions in the show ring. She was the runt of the litter, and the breeder was going to cull her. I got her for nothing, just on the promise I would never let her have pups. She's been a good dog. Always liked kids." His voice dropped on a gravelly note.

Casey glanced at his face, but he'd drawn the hard mask over his rugged features once more. *Better he hides his gentler side today.* Chance's rare tender moods were always her undoing.

Jeannie touched Casey's shoulder. "We're leaving now. Thank you for the wonderful meal. We shouldn't have been away so long, but we had a nice time. Marianne's going to stay on for a while. Maybe one of you can drive her home later."

Rising to walk Jeannie to their pickup, Casey almost offered to drive Marianne home.

Jeannie grasped her hand in a sudden squeeze.

Casey followed her gaze.

Kyle had left the porch to saunter off down to the cottonwood grove.

Beside him, Marianne kept pace with his long, easy strides. Halfway there, the girl stopped to fix the strap on her sandal.

Kyle lifted his hand to cup her elbow while she balanced on one foot. For a moment, their gazes met, and when they finally moved on, their arms remained linked together.

Jeannie breathed a wistful sigh.

Casey's mind eased. "So, it's been Kyle all this time. Somehow, I thought..." She left her own silly imaginings unspoken. "You were talking about Kyle the other day, weren't you?"

Jeannie sniffed and nodded. "Marianne has loved

Kyle since she was just a little girl. I'm afraid there will never be another man for her, and I've worried that Kyle would never see how much she cares. But maybe that's changing." Jeannie's eyes shimmered.

"Let's hope so," Casey murmured. "Let's just hope so."

Morly and Jeannie drove away.

Casey gathered up the glasses and carted them back to the kitchen. She washed them and made a few last swipes at the counter with a sponge.

Chance strolled in. He leaned one hip against the counter edge. "Looks like they've all deserted us. Jamie just took off with Billie and Justin to go for a walk. Even Roy and Ed left with the other wranglers to head into town."

"Did Marianne and Kyle leave, too?" He stood inches from her, and Casey squelched a sudden zing of awareness.

"They left in the SUV. Guess maybe he was taking Marianne home, but she mentioned going for a ride up to Togwotee Pass first."

"Sounds like fun." Casey removed the apron she'd tied over her dress and hung it on a hook inside the cabinet door. "Maybe those two will get together yet."

"Is that what you and Jeannie were whispering about?" Chance leaned past her and lifted the lid from the log cabin cookie jar. "Mmmm, chocolate chip. Billie knows they were always my favorite." He plucked out two cookies and handed one to Casey.

"But guess what?" She accepted the cookie. "I made them. They're Jamie's favorite, too."

Chance took a bite that engulfed half the cookie, and for the first time in days, his eyes glowed with a light that chased away the dark storm clouds. "I can see why. They are mighty tasty." As he chewed and swallowed, his gaze skimmed over Casey.

His eyes were blue as the July sky, and Casey grew warm at their unabashed scrutiny. Frissons of awareness tingled across her skin.

"So, you think my brother and Marianne would make a good pair. Wonder what Kyle thinks about that?" He ate the rest of the cookie.

Unable to swallow, Casey set her cookie on the counter and turned away. "I think if he had half a brain, he would have figured out long ago how she feels." To escape the tension, she headed for the kitchen door.

"I suppose." Chance shifted away from the counter and followed Casey out to the porch.

She stood with him for a moment, taking in the peaceful serenity of the clear summer day. Without any guests and the usual weekday hubbub, the ranch lay strangely silent. Only the distant lowing of a cow or whicker of a horse drifted on the westerly breeze.

"Maybe we ought to take everyone's example and go for a drive ourselves. I know the park is crowded, but you did want to see the historic sites. The lakes are beautiful on a day like this, and I haven't seen them myself in a long time. I'd…like to share them with you, Casey."

She glimpsed again the fleeting warmth and gentleness Chance was so capable of showing but expressed so little. More than anything, Casey wanted to say yes, wanted to spend time with him, savor this lovely summer day, and get to know him better. Maybe not the wisest thing; she would leave in another month, and he would be out of her life forever.

She glanced toward the beckoning mountains beyond the ranch and then back at Chance. "Be ready in a jiffy."

Chapter 10

"I'm sure Aunt Billie will look after Jamie, but I'll leave her a note. I just want to run down to the cabin and change." Casey still wore the sundress and sandals, probably not the outfit for sightseeing. "It won't take me a minute."

"No, don't." Chance halted her. He rested a hand on her arm before sliding it down to grasp her fingers. "You're just fine like this, and it's seldom enough I get to appreciate a woman in a dress. Although." He glanced down at her sandals. "You might want to wear your running shoes."

"With a dress?" Casey made a face.

"Sure, why not? I'll meet you at Billie's cabin. Roy gave me the keys to Juanita, so no riding in the pickup today."

Casey gave in without an argument, but when Chance stopped at the cabin, she noticed he had some trouble climbing out of the four-wheel drive vehicle Roy had affectionately named Juanita. "If your knee is bothering you, I can drive. I've never driven one of these before, but I'm sure—"

"Nothing doing, lady." Chance came around to help her slide up into the high seat. Then he folded his tall frame behind the steering wheel. "No offense, but Juanita is a stick, too, and she might get a little fussy if you're driving."

"What do you mean? You were only with me once when I was driving…" She stopped to consider this. "Ah, so is that why you asked me to let you out two miles from the ranch house? You didn't like the way I drove?"

He glanced from beneath the brim of the hat he'd settled low on his forehead. "It had nothing to do with that. What I told you then was true. I needed more time before I faced this place again."

Casey settled into the bucket seat. "I thought maybe you weren't going to show up at all. Were you that unsure about coming home?"

He paused in starting the engine. "I almost didn't finish that trip down the driveway. I had a mighty strong urge to just head back to the highway."

"But you did come back. I know you still have your differences, but your homecoming has been good medicine for Justin. Probably the best. I think in time you'll find some common ground."

Chance gave a short laugh. "Ah, Casey, the eternal optimist."

"Is there something wrong with that?" Her heart skipped a beat when he sent her one of those darn sexy winks.

"Not a dang thing, and anyway, today I'm glad I did come back."

Casey smiled with satisfaction.

They stopped first at Moose, on the banks of the Snake River. While strolling among the reconstructed buildings of a nineteenth-century homestead, Casey indulged the part of herself that so loved anything to do with the country's history. They wandered from the three-room cabin—one of the original buildings—to the smokehouse, storehouse, the well, and the ferry, while Chance told her about their history.

"A drover from Kansas by the name of Bill Menor built the ferry. The Snake was hazardous, and the ferry became the main crossing point for settlers in this part of Wyoming. Like us, most folks lived on the east side of the river, and they crossed on the ferry to do things like hunt, pick wild berries, or cut wood. Eventually, the ferry carried the visitors who became the first dudes to stay at the ranches near the Tetons. The village of Menor's Ferry sprang up. Later, they renamed it Moose."

They followed the path toward the river. Casey stopped just above the riverbank and stared down into the gray-green water that flowed by in a rushing torrent. "The current is so swift here. I'm sure the settlers were thankful for Bill running the ferry."

"Oh, I don't know. From things I've read, old Bill was a bit of a salty character and not renowned for his gentle nature. It's said he could wither the trees on both banks with his cursing. Especially when the ferry got swept downriver."

Casey tipped her face up at Chance. He made the history of the valley come alive so easily. "A runaway ferry. How the heck did he catch it?"

"Probably got caught on a gravel bar." Chance studied the river. "They say Menor finally got tired of the whole thing and sold out the operation, left Wyoming, and lit out for California."

Chance knew so much about Jackson Hole, and his telling fascinated Casey. But wasn't it a contradiction to the life he'd led? "You don't sound like somebody who wanted to get away from this place."

He shrugged and kicked at a stone. "I always liked knowing what happened in the past, when my great-great-grandparents first homesteaded here. I guess what I didn't want was the responsibility of carrying on the legacy."

She'd never had a deep desire to take over running the farm back home. Thank goodness, Jim had done it. "What happened to the ferry after Menor sold out?"

"Maud Noble bought the operation. She doubled the prices, hoping to make a living from the growing traffic. Then the settlers built a bridge, and they didn't need the ferry anymore." Chance slipped his hand over Casey's, enfolding it in his rough, warm grasp. They followed the trail along the Snake River toward another cabin. He nodded toward the small building. "This was Maud's cabin."

"You should have been a history teacher or a tour guide maybe. You have such a nice way of talking about all this." She swept her free arm around to encompass the path and the river and the cabins. "I'm sure others would like to know the history from someone who grew up in this valley."

He stopped and, still holding her hand, stepped closer. "You mean instead of becoming a rounder and a rodeo man?"

Casey searched his face. His hat brim, as usual, shadowed his expression. She was tempted to reach up and take his hat off to get a better look at what emotion reflected in his eyes right now. Was he serious or in a joking mood? Not one for bold gestures, she just lowered her gaze to focus on the pearl snaps of his shirt. "I guess, if that's what you needed to do, then you shouldn't feel any remorse."

"Even if it upset my family?"

She'd upset her own family by choosing to attend college several hundred miles away from home. Mom, Daddy, and Jim hadn't thought this trip to Wyoming a good idea, either, and tried hard to talk her out of it. What if she'd listened? *I wouldn't be standing in this spot today, with amazing mountains in the background, and a very handsome cowboy in front of me.* "I guess I've done some upsetting in my life, too," she admitted. "My mother calls me every day and asks when I'm coming back to Michigan."

A few seconds slipped by. A small breeze blew past them.

Chance brushed away a few strands of hair that drifted across her face. "So, when are you?"

Maybe never. Did his touch or her unspoken answer set her heart to thumping? "Jamie starts school right after Labor Day. We need to be home before that. My leave from work ends about the same time."

He nodded and tucked her hand into the crook of his elbow. "Guess that means we should make the best of today and whatever time you have here."

At the chapel on the trail, they joined the other tourists inside. Casey loved the simple beauty of the rustic building. The pews were built of quaking aspen. A window framed the Tetons for a perfect backdrop. The peaceful surroundings filled her heart with a sense of coming home. She would have a hard time leaving this valley come end of summer; so much was here to miss. The sound of the wind as it blew through the cottonwoods and the pungent scent of the sage. The way the sky glittered like sapphire above the mountains one minute and turned all misty the next. The stars that

117

twinkled like thousands of sparkling crystals and flung themselves in wild abandon across the vast western night. The bright colors of the scarlet Indian Paintbrush and the deep purple-blue Lupine. The music of a harmonica as it drifted across the pastures and talked to the coyotes and the lowing cows, lulling them to sleep with its soft lonely song. The way a certain man looked at her with strange haunting shadows in his stormy eyes. She would never forget any of this, because it had somehow become a part of her.

Before they left the chapel, Chance laid one hand over his shirt pocket. Lines of loneliness crossed his face.

His expression showed some emotion Casey couldn't interpret. What was going on in his mind? Seeing him like this filled her with sadness. She strode past him, hoping he didn't see the tears that slipped down her cheeks.

Outside, he caught up and drew her close. "Hey, what's this?" He ran a thumb across her damp cheek. "Is it something I said?"

At a loss to explain—even she didn't understand what had just happened—Casey shook her head. Her hair brushed the rest of the tears away. "It's nothing. Just…me." She made an effort to smile and taking his arm tugged him back to the trail. "Come on, let's go see the rest of the sights."

****

Chance accepted her explanation. Understanding women had never been his strong point. This woman had him baffled in many ways. In some respects, she brought out feelings he'd never had for anyone ever before, and he didn't quite know how to deal with them.

He'd been a loner for a while now, had learned to like it, and change didn't come easy for a man like himself. He wasn't sure he could change, but when he was with Casey, he longed to touch her and keep her close and protected. How she really felt about him, he didn't have a clue. But just for today they could enjoy this time together. Just for today, he would make Casey smile and not let their pasts intervene.

Chapter 11

An hour later, Casey stood at the edge of Jenny Lake. The waters glistened like a glacial jewel at the foot of the Tetons. A few fishing boats sailed on her silvery surface, and the craggy peaks mirrored perfectly in her water. The mountains and the lake were one; both were born of the earth's violence, the mighty upheavals of its crust, and the carving power of its ice. The awesome beauty and powerful grandeur of the scene stole over her, letting her forget for the moment all the pain and heartache of the past three years.

Beside her, Chance lifted his gaze to the mountains.

On the drive to the lake, he had talked about the settling of Jackson Hole, from the mountain men, who were the first white explorers in the valley, to the ones like Chance's ancestors, who had come down the Gros Ventre River to carve out their homesteads on the thick Wyoming grass. His voice held respect, despite reservations about his own life in the valley. "Perhaps you should be the one who helps Justin with his book. It might bring the two of you together." She glanced sideways. How would he take this suggestion? Would coming home to this place give him whatever he was seeking?

Chance chuckled and shook his head. "Still intent on reconciling us McCord men, aren't you? Justin and I are managing. He agreed to my buying some mustangs from the roundups to work with and train. Kyle's not crazy about the idea, but he's being civil about it, and we're tolerating each other. That's about the best we can hope for at this point, and it's good enough for me."

Wandering along the lake, Casey stooped to find delicate forget-me-nots hidden beneath the whitebark pines. The waves slapped gently at the shore, and then a high-pitched cry echoed across the lake. Above them, an eagle spotted an unwary prey and performed an aerial ballet, circling closer and closer to the water, and finally swooping down in a lightning dive and flash of talons to snatch a fish from the lake. With a shriek of victory, the eagle sailed off to enjoy his catch at some mountain lair.

Casey shielded her eyes against the sun and watched the eagle's retreat. "The fishermen have competition."

"But his kind were here first." Chance nodded toward the eagle that was only a dark dot now against the brilliant blue sky.

Casey brought her attention back to the lake, where other visitors were wading in the shallows. "How cold do you think the water is?"

Chance folded his arms and leaned his back against a nearby tree. "You could find out."

She accepted his dare and slipped off her shoes. Holding back her dress with one hand, she waded in but let out a shriek at the shock of the water temperature.

He laughed. "What's the matter? Too cold for you?"

She scooped up a handful of water and tossed it. "Why don't you take off those boots and join me, cowboy?" She dipped her hand into the water again.

He stepped back from the shore. "Not a chance, sweetheart. I used to swim in Jenny Lake. I know how cold it is." Farther on, beside a small pond, Chance pointed out where a beaver had built its dam. "Listen close, and you might hear him slap his tail."

Instead, Casey heard the *rat-a-tat-tat* of a woodpecker in a lodgepole pine and the raucous croaking of a pair of ravens. "Nice background music," she mused.

"I always thought so." Chance guided her along the rest of the trail. "Nature's music. The kind that soothes your soul."

Casey relished the carefree hour spent by Jenny Lake and tucked the music away in her heart. She would always remember this afternoon. She'd learned a lot about Chance today. He wasn't the drifter cowboy she'd first imagined, but someone who appreciated the history and heritage of the valley. Unlike many others, he also believed the original inhabitants of this wild region should have first rights. He wasn't the reckless, rootless man he professed to be. In a way, she wished she hadn't found that out. Knowing Chance better would make leaving that much harder.

At Billie's cabin, Casey asked Chance in for coffee. "I can make us some sandwiches, since we missed dinner."

He took off his hat as they entered the cabin, and his tall frame filled the small front room. Casey's nerves tingled. Outside, his closeness didn't affect her nearly so much.

Billie and Jamie were both curled on the old rust-brown sofa, the boy's towhead nestled on Billie's lap.

Wrapped in her plaid robe, Billie dozed, but she roused when Chance and Casey opened the door. "About time you two showed up. Thought maybe you ran off together or something."

"And left Jamie behind?" Casey knelt beside her sleeping son and kissed his head. "Not on your life. But I'm sorry I wasn't here to help you with supper. We drove up to the park, and time slipped away. Did you manage all right?"

Billie stifled a yawn. "Honey, I managed long before you came out here to help, and I plan on doing it for a while longer. Did you have a good time?"

The wealth of understanding Casey read in Billie's brown eyes calmed her. "We did, and thanks for keeping an eye on Jamie. He's going to miss you and Justin."

Billie's eyes misted, but she quickly sniffed away any show of emotion. "How about you take this youngin' off to bed? He beat Justin at three games of checkers in a row and thought he was pretty smart. He wanted to stay awake and tell you, but he just couldn't keep his eyes open. I'm about ready to hit the hay myself. We've got a full house of guests arriving tomorrow."

Casey leaned to lift Jamie from the sofa.

Chance gently shouldered her out of the way and scooped the boy into his arms. He crossed to the bedroom, his boots clunking on the hardwood floor.

Casey hurried ahead and folded back the patchwork quilt on Jamie's cot.

Laying the boy down, Chance hovered over him for a minute. He paused to push back the sweep of pale blond hair from Jamie's forehead. "He's a nice little kid. Too bad his dad didn't get to see him grow up."

"Matt was so proud of him." Casey tucked the quilt around Jamie's shoulders. "I like to think he can still see Jamie." A little catch in her throat tripped up her words. The pain wasn't for herself but for Jamie and what he missed by not having his father.

Chance left the room and grabbed his hat from where he'd left it on a hook by the door. He turned the brim in his hands.

Billie had gone off to bed, and the little cabin was quiet, save for the ticking of the clock.

The evening had grown cooler, and Casey rubbed her arms. "I'll make that coffee and sandwiches. We can sit out on the porch." She turned toward the kitchen.

"That's okay…think I'll head off to the bunkhouse. Tomorrow starts a busy week. My turn to take a group out for a day-long ride up to the canyon. I need to check out the horses they'll ride."

Casey knew Chance didn't relish that job. He would much rather do the ranch work than cater to guests, but he would carry his share.

As he headed for the door, he winced and leaned over to rub his knee.

"Are you sure a day-long ride is a good idea? I'm sure if you asked Kyle, he'd get Roy to do it."

Chance straightened. He turned around and narrowed his eyes. "I didn't come back here to be pampered, Casey, and I sure as heck won't turn my job over to a young wrangler like Roy. I might not be able to do the work I used to, but I won't ask for any quarter, especially not from my kid brother."

Of course, he wouldn't. "You don't have to prove

yourself, you know."

Silence fell for a second, and he blew out a heavy sigh. "Yeah, I kinda do."

She followed him out to the porch and inhaled the cool night air. How did she always manage to say the wrong thing? Why was it so difficult to understand where he was coming from? She gripped the railing for support. He could arouse such conflicting emotions in her without even trying. If only they could have hung onto the sweet afternoon at Jenny Lake, but perhaps the day had only been a fleeting moment in time—gone like the eagle into the wide-open sky. Which was maybe better anyway.

Chance stood behind her.

Casey closed her eyes. *Please, just let him walk on by.*

He came closer. "We had a nice day together, and I don't want to ruin it. But we have a lot of problems to work through. You're not ready for something more than a walk by the lake, and maybe I'm not either, but we can't deny what's between us. I know you feel it, too." He put his hands on her shoulders and slid them down her arms. "You're cold. Best go on inside. We'll talk another time. I have some things to tell you."

As she had things to tell him.

He went past her and down the steps.

Her heart sank lower in her chest.

Then, as if he remembered something, he came back.

Standing on the top step, Casey was eye level with him.

He curved his hand behind her neck and drew her close.

The touch of his lips on hers burned hot like the first spark of a wildfire that might ignite a prairie blaze. Like a spark that burst into flame in the face of a fierce summer wind, the kiss grew more intense until Casey feared the passion would consume her.

In the next breath, Chance was gone.

Casey touched her trembling lips. How could she ever fall for such a man? He was nothing like Matt, was maybe not a good example for Jamie, and yet, as surely as snow fell on the mountains come autumn and the valley turned winter white, she was falling in love.

****

The following week, a new group of guests descended on the ranch and kept everyone hopping. Casey didn't mind. While cleaning the cabins, she stayed too busy to dwell on the walk by Jenny Lake. As she plumped the pillows on the bed in the last cabin of the day, she heard someone tap on the screen door.

"It's just me. Marianne. You got a minute?"

"Sure. Come on in." Casey blew back a few errant strands of hair that escaped her bandanna. She gave the red-and-white calico quilt a final pat and straightened rubbing her back. Thank goodness she was almost finished for the day. She met Marianne in the front room. "Whew. Tucking in all these sheets and blankets can be hard on the old spine. I'm glad there are only six cabins. I think I've had it today."

"I know what you mean," Marianne commiserated. "Mom's left cleaning the guest cabins to me this summer. I don't mind, but it can get a little backbreaking."

"And you're ten years younger." Casey groaned and waved to the two wingback chairs that made up the small sitting area of the cabin. "Let's sit down. I could use a breather. Once I'm done here, I promised Aunt Billie I'd make a couple of pies for dinner tonight." She dropped into one of the chairs and pulled off the bandanna, patting at the perspiration beading on her upper lip.

Marianne hesitated, then perched on the arm of the other chair. She fidgeted and plucked at her hair that fell in two dark braids today.

Casey leaned toward her. She had a pretty good idea what troubled the younger woman. "So, what's up?"

"I…guess you saw me…with Kyle last Sunday." She twisted the end of one braid around her finger. "He drove me home later, and we're supposed to get our group of guests together for a steak fry down by the river. Has he mentioned it?"

"He was talking about it with a couple of the fellas at lunch today. Sounds like fun, and I'm sure my son will love it." Casey paused a minute. "If you need help with the cooking, I'll volunteer."

"That'd be great. Then Mom and Dad could have a little time to themselves. The thing I was wondering is…" Marianne took a deep breath and looked Casey square in the eye. "This probably sounds stupid, but does Kyle ever talk about me? I mean, does he ever mention me at all? I know you've only been here a short time, and this might sound presumptuous, but I just really need to know…where I stand with him. I can't ask anyone else."

Hopeful expectation dwelled in Marianne's hazel eyes, and Casey's heart filled with empathy. She remembered what it was like to love someone and not

127

be sure of how he felt. Before Matt ever professed his love she'd done her share of worrying. Even now, her feelings for Chance presented a giant uncertainty in her life. "You care about Kyle a lot, don't you?"

Marianne dropped her gaze to her hands clasped together now in her lap. "Does it show so much? I don't want to make a fool of myself, but I love Kyle. I always have and always will, but if I can't have him, I won't waste my life wanting him."

"Your mom would be happy to hear that. She's worried about you."

"You mean my mother knows?" Marianne lifted her eyebrows.

"Don't look so surprised. Mother's intuition isn't a joke. About Kyle, I wish I could tell you, but I seldom see him except at meals. He's always so concerned with ranch business, and he talks of little else. But, judging by the way he acted with you Sunday, he's definitely interested. Maybe it's just taking him awhile to realize it."

"I don't know how long I can wait." Marianne sprang from the arm of the chair and paced the small room. "I've applied for a couple of teaching positions, not in the valley, and I should be hearing on them soon. I just wish I knew how that darn cowboy feels before I leave." She stopped at the door and gazed out at the mountains rising in the distance. "We just never have enough time. I had hoped with Chance home things would change, and Kyle would have more free time for us to, you know, hang out together. But it doesn't seem as though Chance wants any part of running the ranch. I guess he never did want the responsibility."

"I think it's mutual." Casey rose to Chance's

defense. "I don't believe Kyle wants his brother taking over. A lot of bitterness still holds those two apart."

"With good cause!" Marianne swung back around. "What happened was a terrible thing, but I never believed any of what they said about Kyle."

Casey pressed her lips together. Was she close to discovering what divided the two brothers? Suddenly, she had to know. Maybe then she'd understand the reason for the McCord family's disharmony and the reason why Chance held himself apart. "What didn't you believe?"

Marianne glanced away. "It's nothing. I…I shouldn't have said that. It's just I'm so mixed up right now."

She wasn't the only one. Yet as much as Casey liked the younger woman, she couldn't pour out her own bewildered feelings. Neither could she give any sensible advice right now other than, "Give it a little more time. If you and Kyle are supposed to be together, it'll work out."

"I wish I could be as sure as you are." Marianne managed an unconvincing smile. "I'm not a very patient person."

Casey joined Marianne at the door. "I wasn't either at your age. I could hardly wait for Matt to propose. I practically asked him myself."

Marianne tipped her head to one side and studied Casey. "Mom told me you're a widow. I guess that's hard, especially having a child."

"Losing Matt was hard." Casey blew out a bittersweet sigh. "Sometimes, it still is, but I picked myself up and went on, because I had to. That's what Matt would expect."

"Do you think you'll ever marry again?"

The question jolted Casey. She'd not given much thought to the possibility. Up until now no man could take Matt's place. "I don't know. Maybe. If the right guy came along."

"Would Chance be the right guy?"

The girl had no qualms about speaking her mind, but Casey couldn't admit what she felt or didn't feel for such a complicated man. Least of all, she couldn't admit anything to Marianne. Gossip spread like a grassfire around the valley, and besides, the girl seemed to bear a grudge against Chance; a grudge that had to do with whatever happened to drive the two brothers apart.

"I hardly know Chance." Casey made an effort to quell the idea in Marianne's mind. "Jamie likes him, and he's very sweet and gentle with my son. But between us, it's nothing more than friendship." Had her nose grown longer with that lie?

A knowing grin crossed Marianne's face. "You rode with him to our place that afternoon and went off together last Sunday. You were still gone when we got back."

"We spent a couple of afternoons together." Casey sought to make light of Marianne's observations. "Chance offered to show me some of the sights in the park. Doesn't mean we have a relationship."

Marianne nodded. At a ding, she grabbed her phone from her jeans pocket. "Guess I better get home. Mom expects me to help with dinner." Just before she left, Marianne paused at the door. A tiny frown marred her forehead. "You're right about Chance being gentle, but you should know, his kind never truly settles down.

Once rodeo is in their blood, cowboys like Chance always have an itch to go on down the road. He's been that way ever since I can remember. I doubt he'll ever change."

"Don't you believe people can start over?" Casey refused to let Marianne think she had doubts about the man. "Perhaps he wants to change."

"Even if he does, you're a person who deserves better." A sad smile crossed her face as she shook her head. "Take my word for it, Casey. He'll only hurt you."

Casey didn't thank her for the warning but turned back to tidying the cabin.

Marianne left without offering any further advice.

How ironic the girl had wanted some words of wisdom and ended up giving them herself. But were they true? It would hardly seem so coming from someone so young, but the Hansons had known Chance for a long time. Probably they all knew about the "terrible thing" that had driven a spike of mistrust down the center of the McCord family.

A thousand and one reasons existed why she should believe what Marianne told her, but in her heart, Casey believed people had the right to turn their lives around.

Chapter 12

The long strip of Wyoming highway shimmered in the summer sun, and the truck tires hummed. Chance kept his gaze fixed straight ahead and on the alert for wildlife crossing the road in the Hoback Mountains.

Roy drummed his fingers on his knee to the beat of a song on the radio. "How come you didn't ask Kyle to go with you?"

The younger wrangler agreed to travel to Rock Springs to pick up a couple of mustang colts at the holding pens. He figured Roy was glad to get away from the ranch for the day.

"My brother had more important stuff to do. Besides, Kyle's not exactly in favor of this whole idea."

"But Justin is."

Over the summer, Chance had learned how much the wranglers respected Justin, and he didn't want to destroy Roy's relationship with him. But maybe Roy should know some of what had driven the McCord men apart. "My father and I rarely see eye-to-eye. So while he's not crazy about wild horses at the ranch, I guess maybe he figures if I have a reason to stay at the North Star, I won't up and disappear again."

The radio station faded. Roy fiddled with the knobs. "Your absence was tough on him. Even before he got sick."

Chance nodded in recognition of that fact. "How

long have you worked at the ranch?"

"Almost five years."

As long as I was gone. "You probably think I'm a selfish jerk for staying away like I did."

A country song blared from the speakers. Roy tipped his hat down and shifted to stare out the passenger window. "Not for me to judge. I've stayed away from my own family for a while now. We all got our reasons."

Chance might have told Roy the reason why he'd left in the first place, but he spotted a couple of mule deer sprinting across the highway ahead. He slowed and scanned the side of the road.

A doe and her two fawns scampered after the rest.

They drove on a few more miles.

"How many horses are we picking up?" Roy asked.

"Four to start. Two Pintos and two Appaloosas rounded up out of the Red Desert. I'll see how it goes training them before I plan for more. Justin's given me the use of the north pasture. They've not had cattle in it for a few years." Chance waited a minute. "I understand you've got experience working with mustangs. Ed mentioned it."

"My dad worked with wild horses when I was a kid. He taught me a thing or two."

"I've seen you with the horses on the ranch. You know what you're doing. Want to give me a hand working with this group? I can always use another cowboy's advice." He sent a quick glance over to Roy.

The wrangler lifted one shoulder in a slight shrug. "Kyle keeps me busy. I got plenty of work to do."

"I would never ask you to slack on that. Just thought maybe if you had some spare time, we could work together." He held up one hand. "But hey, no pressure. I'm sure you've got a life outside of the ranch."

"Truth is, I don't leave the ranch much in the summer."

Chance chuckled. "What, no girl in town? On another ranch? Back home?" Roy's moment of hesitation spoke more than any words of denial, and Chance regretted the offhand remark. Maybe for the wrangler there'd been someone, someone who couldn't deal with his line of work, someone who'd dumped him or, like himself, had been tragically lost. "Sorry, don't mean to pry. Anyway, if you've got time, I'd appreciate whatever advice you can give me. I worked for a guy who believed in giving these horses a life that's worthwhile, a second chance, instead of penning them up for years. It seems like a good purpose for my life right now." Did that pique the wrangler's interest?

Roy faced Chance, his dark eyes intense. "I respect that belief. I can help you."

Chance took his right hand from the steering wheel and offered it to Roy. "Thanks. We'll work something out. Like I said, it won't take away from your regular chores. I've got my own. When I came home, I never expected any special treatment because of who I am. I still don't."

Roy shook his hand.

In that moment, Chance glimpsed a hint of something different in the wrangler's expression. Respect maybe? Not a bad thing to have from another cowboy. Maybe even the beginning of a friendship.

A few days later, Chance and Roy finished their first lesson with the young mustangs. Chance noticed

Casey and Jamie had wandered down to the corral to watch and motioned them over to the gate. He hadn't talked to Casey since the day they walked by Jenny Lake, but the memory of their kiss at the end of the day lingered. He'd give anything for another moment like that one.

"Hi, Chance!" Jamie hung on the fence rails and waved. "We came to see the new horses."

Taking off his hat, Chance brushed the sweat from his forehead and meandered to the gate. He tried not to favor his bum knee. Even if he wasn't quite sure of what to say, the sight of Casey drifted over him like a breath of fresh air on this hot summer day. "So, what do you think of them?" He propped his elbows on the top rail and leaned backwards against the fence. "Do you remember what we call those two?" He nodded toward the red-and-white spotted colts.

"Pintos," Jamie pronounced. "And the other ones are Appaloosas." He flashed a big grin at Chance.

"Nice job." Chance fake-punched the boy and winked at Casey. He saw her cheeks flush a pale pink. At least, he could still affect her in a good way. That was some encouragement. "What have you two been up to lately?" Could he get a few words out of her?

She kept her gaze diverted from his and watched the young mustangs kick up their hooves in play. "Just cooking and cleaning cabins and not much else."

He inclined his head toward her. "Sorry I haven't made it in for dinner this week." More wranglers were hired on in the summer, and Billie sent food down to the bunkhouse kitchen. He'd taken advantage of that, still aiming to be treated as just another cowboy. He liked that setup, except it gave him less opportunity to see Casey. She and Billie were still busy in the big house kitchen.

"But tomorrow, we're gonna watch them cut hay," Jamie chimed in. "Kyle said it's good weather for it."

"Yeah? I used to watch that, too, when I was a kid. Maybe I'll see you down there. They can always use some extra help." He peered up at the clear blue sky overhead. Nary a cloud in sight. "We have to take advantage of the dry weather. I bet that's true on your folks' farm, right, Casey?"

"I'm sure they're cutting hay back home, too."

Her voice held a wistful tone. Did she miss that? Was life on their farm so different from here?

"Taking the colts to the pasture," Roy called out.

Chance nodded and signaled him *I'll be right there.* "So, maybe I'll see you tomorrow. Don't forget water. It gets pretty hot and dry out there in the hayfield." *Come on, Casey, at least look at me. Give me a smile.*

She did, briefly, before getting Jamie down from the fence.

"See you at the hayfield." The boy waved.

Chance waved back as the two made their way to the house. He and Roy herded the young mustangs into another corral.

When they finished, the wrangler wound up the lead ropes. "So, now you're cutting hay?" Roy's dark eyes pinned him.

"Yeah, well, like I said, they can always use an extra hand." Chance secured the gate and coughed a bit from the dust the horses had stirred up. "And afterwards, I can explain it all to Jamie."

"And his mom?"

He looked forward to stealing a moment alone with

her and maybe figuring out what had changed. "I'm sure Casey will be there. She doesn't let that boy out of her sight for very long."

"Except for that day the two of you went for a ride."

Chance turned away from the corral, but not from Roy. Usually, the wrangler didn't have a whole lot to say, pretty much kept his own confidence and his nose out of other people's business. "What're you getting at?"

From beneath the brim of his hat, Roy's dark eyes glittered. "Just think the mustangs aren't the only reason you'll be staying on at the North Star."

The wrangler's words stuck with Chance all that night and kept him awake until the early morning hours, when the sky above the Tetons glimmered pink. If Casey stayed, would he? The day by Jenny Lake had left him with a deep longing. They stepped back from each other at the end of the day, both unsure of how they felt, but there was that kiss. She didn't protest that, nor the ones before, and she kissed him back. So, why today did Casey ignore him? What had happened?

Leaving the bunkhouse before anyone else, he headed out to do morning chores. The questions still churned in his mind. When would Casey leave the ranch? And more importantly, did he need to get any more involved than he already was? For sure, neither of them needed more heartache in their lives, so maybe he should keep his distance. Let her go back to Michigan and find a better man. As he filled a water trough outside one of the barns, Chance convinced himself this was for the best.

The following day, Casey drove the truck, parking

it beneath a grove of cottonwoods, and she and Jamie watched the cutting process from a safe distance.

From his seat on the tractor, Chance noticed how her long hair caught back in a ponytail left her face open to the breeze. She lifted her chin, maybe to appreciate the sweet scent of the freshly cut hay. He imagined her gray eyes scanning over the fields, taking in the valley and the mountains beyond. *Those gray eyes.* From that moment at the café, her eyes captured his attention.

Finished for the afternoon, he glanced over at the truck. She still sat cross-legged on the open tailgate. The boy wasn't anywhere around. He threw his earlier conviction aside and approached the truck. "Jamie give up on hay cutting?"

"He was hungry. Billie came and got him. And anyway, he had a date with Justin for a game of checkers." She opened a small cooler behind her and took out a thermos, handing it to Chance. "It's lemonade. Should still be cold."

He took the thermos and screwed open the top, not bothering to pour the lemonade into the cup but just drinking straight from the container. The cold, tangy liquid slid down his parched throat, washing away the dust from the hay. "Thank you. I finished my water a long time ago." He parked his backside against the tailgate. "How come you stayed out here?" He wished she'd say *to see you.*

A shadow passed over Casey's face, and tears hovered on her lashes.

His belly clutched tight. "Is something wrong?"

She swiped her eyes with her fingers. "I just needed to get away for a little while. It's kind of nice sitting out here, even if it's hot."

He didn't press her to say more but sat with her while a magpie flew overhead and a meadowlark called out.

But then Casey sniffed.

He tossed aside his caution. "Anything I can help with?" Did he dare take her hand? "If it's none of my business—"

"No, it's okay. I just…before I drove down here today, I had a conversation with my mother." She pressed her lips together and frowned. "She called—again—to ask when I'm coming home."

"And that upset you? I thought you said she calls you every day."

She sniffed a little louder and slid closer, resting her head on his shoulder. "She thinks I'm a terrible mother. That I'm doing Jamie a grave disservice by keeping him out here away from his family." Her voice broke. "That I'm depriving him—"

"Whoa, whoa now." Chance held up one hand. "Nothing against your family, Casey, but that's nonsense, and you know it. Jamie is anything but deprived. I haven't seen a kid so happy. He's like a young pig in slop."

She laughed, cried a little more, then lifted her head, but she didn't move away. "Gee thanks. So now my son's a pig?"

Chance nudged her shoulder. "You know what I mean. He's got his mom who loves him, a ranch full of animals, and a bunch of other people happy to keep him busy. What else does he need?"

She fished a tissue from her pocket and dabbed at her eyes. "I know. I'm a thirty-two-year-old woman, but my mom can make me feel so…inadequate. It's always been that way."

"Seriously? You, inadequate? Casey, honey, look at me."

She lifted her misty gray gaze.

He was close to taking her in his arms and kissing away all the sadness, but a bad move could injure a tender heart even more. Hurting Casey was the last thing he wanted to do. "You can't let it get to you. If anybody knows about dealing with a judgmental family, it's me. I let it rule my life for far too long, and now I'm done with it. I think you've probably been through enough, too. Let it go, Casey. If just for today, let it go." Seeing her lips curve into a tiny smile hit him like a sucker punch. He wanted to taste those lips again. But not today.

"Thank you," she whispered. "That means a lot."

"Hey, it's the least I can do for a girl who gave a down-and-out-cowboy a ride. Speaking of which, how about giving him a ride again? I think the rest of the crew left, and I've got some horses to feed."

Casey unfolded herself and slid from the tailgate. "Sure enough, partner, but only if you don't make fun of how I drive."

Before he got into the truck, Chance stood by the passenger side door. "What did you tell your mother?"

Casey paused, hand on the ignition key. "That I'm not leaving yet. Because I'm not ready."

He said nothing more, just nodded and climbed into the truck. What more could he say to make Casey feel better? He wasn't sure his advice was helpful, but at the moment, it was the best he could do.

Chapter 13

"Hurry up, Mom, or they'll leave us behind." Jamie jumped around the bedroom, his boots clunking on the floor. "Kyle said we gotta be ready by five."

"Since it's only four thirty, I don't think we have to worry. Besides, I'm running the chuckwagon. I doubt they'll leave without me." Casey tied a jaunty red scarf at her neck and slicked sheer pink gloss over her lips to keep them from chapping in the dry air. She ran the brush through her hair one more time and checked her image in the mirror. The scarf set off her stone-washed jeans and blue chambray shirt with embroidery at the yoke. The new turquoise-blue boots she'd bought this past week boasted a nice shine. *Perfect outfit for a trail ride and steak fry.* She tucked the lip gloss into her jeans pocket. "How do I look?" She turned for her son's approval.

Jamie wrinkled his nose.

"What? Not so good?" She flicked a glance in the mirror again.

"I hope you're not wearing any of that smelly perfume." He groaned. "The horses won't like it."

"My perfume is not smelly." Casey picked up the spray bottle of scent she often wore. "It's called Summer Breeze. But okay, Mr. Smarty Pants, you win. I won't wear any perfume tonight. We wouldn't want to upset the horses." She put the bottle back on the dresser and picked up a blue quilted vest for herself and a denim jacket for Jamie. "I'm ready."

At the bedroom door, Jamie hesitated. He looked up at Casey. "Did Dad like it? The perfume, I mean."

Casey paused. They hadn't talked about Matt in a while. "I used to wear that perfume because he liked it. The scent reminded him of blue skies and warm July days." She'd worn it the night he asked her to marry him and every day after until just recently. She wasn't sure why she packed the perfume for the trip to Wyoming.

Jamie slouched his shoulders. "Do you think he's happy without us? Does he miss us?" He chewed his bottom lip.

Casey swallowed a lump in her throat. She didn't need to start the evening on a sad note, but Jamie deserved an honest answer. "I'm sure he does, as we miss him, but I think he's happy. He was a good man, and I believe he's in Heaven now."

Jamie sniffed and rubbed his nose. "I still miss him sometimes." His gaze dropped to his boots.

She allowed him to hide his emotions. Even little boys possessed a certain amount of manly pride. "So do I, Jamie, but knowing he's happy takes away some of the hurt." She gave his shoulders a quick hug.

He hesitated from moving away. "Is Chance a good man, Mom? He's been nice, teaching me to ride, and never gettin' mad if I ask him lots of stuff. Does that count?"

Casey read the need on her son's face to hear her say Chance was the man he wanted him to be. How did she explain sometimes people lost their way, and it took a while to get back on track again? How did she explain a man like Chance McCord when she didn't understand him herself? Her thoughts flashed to last week at the hayfield. Chance did what he could to make her feel better and didn't ask for anything. "It counts," she said softly.

Jamie hugged her around the middle. "I guess if Dad liked your perfume...then you should wear it." He dashed off. "Beat you to the barn!"

Casey watched him go. So cute the way her son showed affection one minute and then acted embarrassed the next. He was so typically male. Before leaving the bedroom, she went to the dresser and lifted the bottle of perfume. She gave herself a light spray.

In the cabin kitchen, Billie glanced up from a huge picnic basket. She'd nursed a summer cold this past week and decided not to attend the steak fry. She and Casey had done some of the cooking here at the cabin, and Billie finished packing the basket. "What were you two chattering about?"

"Jamie just asked me some things." Casey put a pot of baked beans and two loaves of crusty bread into the basket, followed by veggie strips and a covered pan of chocolate cupcakes. "He told me not to wear any perfume, and then he wanted to know if Matt is happy without us." She smiled at the two notions that were so unrelated.

Billie shook her head. "I'm not even going to ask for an explanation of that. I remember how a little boy's mind works."

Gripping the handles of the basket, Casey studied Billie's careworn face. "I hope you're not going back to the big house tonight. I'm sure Justin can manage by himself. You should get some extra rest."

"I plan on it." Billie pulled a tissue from a nearby box and blew her nose. "I left some supper for Justin, and the fellas not going to the steak fry said they'd eat in town tonight."

"That's good to hear." Casey leaned over and pecked a kiss on Billie's soft cheek. "You work too hard."

"Nonsense. If it wasn't for this lousy cold, I'd be out there doing all this."

"I'm sure you'd be right in the middle, calling all the shots." She clutched the picnic basket and escaped out the door before Billie could scold.

She hoisted the basket under her arm and set out for the corral. Would Chance join the cookout tonight? Despite the precarious state of their relationship, she'd welcome his company. But then, he wasn't always thrilled about joining in the group activities. Maybe he'd hide out somewhere. Or take a solo ride. Wouldn't surprise her. She hoped he could set aside the issues with his brother for one night and enjoy himself. Maybe even spend a few moments alone with her. Was it too much to hope for?

****

Chance slammed the door of the bunkhouse and jammed on his hat. Grumbling, he strode out to the barn. His decision to go on the trail ride rankled him; he would've much preferred to spend the evening alone. Or maybe gone over the pass to the Wrangler's Roost for a couple of cold ones.

He and Justin had talked earlier, and the discussion hadn't gone well. His father was in a cantankerous mood. Determined Chance take more interest in the business of the North Star, he rambled on about some upcoming cattle auction. Chance was just as determined to keep things as they were, with himself working like any other ranch hand and Kyle in charge. The old man didn't understand any better than he did years ago what made his older son tick, and Chance was at a loss to explain. And so, they were at loggerheads. Would the situation ever work itself out? Probably not, and the disagreement left Chance with a hot knot of tension in the pit of his stomach. The last thing he wanted was to put on a cheerful face for the guests, but he'd told Kyle he would drive the chuck wagon. He didn't owe his brother anything, but maybe he owed it to himself to take some responsibility for running the ranch. Even if it grated against his stubborn nature like salt on an open wound, he would keep his word.

****

Near the barns, Casey noticed Chance adjusting the harness on the draft horses that would pull the chuck wagon. A little thrill of excitement shot through her veins. Straightening her shoulders, she tamped down her nerves and approached him.

One of the horses nickered.

Chance glanced up. "Hey, Casey. I heard you're doing the cooking tonight. The guys are all pretty excited about the menu."

She stopped beside him. "Billie and I've been cooking all day. We even have chocolate cupcakes and cherry cobbler for dessert." She bent to set the heavy basket on the ground, but the horse nearest her nudged her shoulder, and she almost lost her grip.

In a lightning quick move, Chance caught the basket and lifted it from her arms. "I'll stick this in the wagon." He carried it around the back.

"Thanks." She followed him. "Where's Kyle? Is he coming, too? Marianne will be awfully disappointed if he doesn't." Better to keep the conversation about somebody else.

A grin tugged at the corners of Chance's mouth. "Don't worry. He'll be along in a minute. He had to take a phone call about some livestock he's buying at auction."

Casey checked out the wagon with its various drawers and compartments, high narrow wheels, and assortment of black kettles and pots. "Billie says the wagon is reminiscent of those used on the long cattle drives in the 1800s. I think you could carry a little bit of everything in here." She peered inside the wagon. "I can't imagine cooking out of such a contraption. It all looks very efficient for the time, but it couldn't have been easy."

Chance made room for the basket of food next to a big cooler. "Probably wasn't, but the cook on a trail drive was an important man. He fed the drovers during the months on the trail and served as doctor for the men and horses. He even cut hair and pulled teeth."

"Let's hope I'm not called on to perform any of those duties. Afraid I'd have to bow out." Casey watched Chance as he walked around the team of matching bay draft horses, checking their harness. "By the way, who's driving this rig down to the river?" Was that Kyle's job, or would he relegate the responsibility to a wrangler? Roy maybe?

Chance adjusted the harness collars on the team. "Looks like yours truly."

Casey smiled to herself. Was this his idea, or had Kyle asked him? It didn't matter. Her pulse quickened at the thought of sitting beside Chance on the wagon. She'd missed him these past few busy days.

"Come say hello to Mac and Red." Chance motioned her toward the head of the team. "I don't think you've met them yet."

"But who's who?" She stood beside the horse that had nudged her and reached to stroke his muscular, dark brown shoulder.

"That is Mac." Chance pointed to the harness collars. "Their names are engraved on their collars. Mac has a wider blaze on his face, but otherwise yeah, it's hard to tell them apart. They're a matched team."

Mac pressed his velvety nose against her shoulder and blew gently.

The warm breath tickled her neck. Casey laughed. "They look very sweet, but they're huge." She patted Red, who nuzzled her for his share of attention.

"They're Belgians and gentle as lambs. Here, give me your hands, palms up." He dropped two sugar cubes in them, then held her hands out for the giants to lip the treats. "Keep them flat, and they won't hurt you." While Mac and Red crunched, Chance still held her hands, running his thumbs over her palms.

Casey cleared her throat and dared to glance up. The look in his sultry eyes said *kiss me*, and she gladly would have, but two kids ran past, bumping into them.

"Hey, kids, no running by the horses," he called out. He turned back, but the moment had passed. "Time to get everybody saddled up. You can wait by the wagon and keep an eye on the team now you've made friends." He winked.

Casey subdued a pleasurable sigh.

He started to leave but stopped and drew a folded

piece of paper from his shirt pocket. "Almost forgot, here's the list of guests Kyle gave me. So you know who's who on the ride. I'll be back shortly."

She watched him leave, noticing how he tried very hard not to limp. *Men.* She'd never understand them. She opened the note. Three families were going on the ride tonight—the Richardsons from Iowa, the Millers from New York, and a pair of newlyweds, Bob and Janet Flaherty, from Wisconsin. All but the Flahertys had children of various ages, which delighted Jamie. He'd had a wonderful time with the other kids all week and whooped and ran around with them, as if he didn't have a care in the world. Apparently, he'd forgotten the earlier conversation about Matt. Thank goodness, children were so resilient.

Chance and Roy selected horses geared to their guests' riding ability. They put the children on thoroughly trained trail horses; the ones who would just plod along in follow-the-leader fashion. A few of the adults had a bit more riding experience, but even their horses were well-trained.

Would the young mustangs Chance had brought to the ranch one day take their place as trail horses? Casey knew that was his hope, but the reality lay a long way down the road. The better question was, would training the mustangs keep Chance at the North Star?

Jamie scrambled up in Buckwheat's saddle. "Here comes Kyle!" He pointed toward the house.

Kyle approached the buckskin he always rode. Astride Ranger, he took his place at the head of the group.

He looked very handsome in a tan Western shirt with pearl snaps and a dark brown hat. Dark brown cord jeans had replaced the usual denim ones, and even his boots, though worn down at the heel, were shinier than usual. The other wranglers were spiffed up, too, but did Kyle hope to impress someone tonight?

Much the same as he always did, Chance wore jeans faded to a soft pale blue and a rumpled plaid shirt with the sleeves rolled back. His black hat, the weather-beaten one he wore that first day she met him in the café, tipped down and shadowed his face. In his case, clothes didn't make the man. The man was too virile to begin with, and even dressed in a formal tux, Chance would exude the same rugged quality. The mental image of Chance in a tux made Casey chuckle.

He climbed onto the wagon seat. "May I ask what's so funny?" As he picked up the harness lines, he brushed his arm against hers.

She would never tell him, and he'd never follow her train of thought. "I guess I'm just happy tonight. It's a beautiful evening, and I think this is going to be great fun." She didn't add his company helped her upbeat attitude.

"You must've not talked to your mother today."

She tossed her head. "Actually, I did, but I took your advice and let it all go once we hung up."

He nodded. "Good girl. Now you're learning." A twinkle sparkled in his eyes.

The first bump on the trail bounced her against his shoulder. Casey grabbed his knee for support but quickly snatched her hand away.

"You can leave it there. I should've warned you how bumpy this old wagon is. If you wanted to ride, I could've given you Dakota."

"I'm fine." She gripped the wagon seat instead.

Chance clucked to the horses, and they picked up their pace.

The trail widened, and the chuck wagon brought up the rear of the group. Casey watched the other riders and tried to catch a glimpse of Jamie. Was someone keeping an eye on him?

"Don't worry. He's fine."

She glanced at Chance.

He kept his gaze straight ahead.

She settled back to enjoy the ride. Quivering aspen trees lined the trail, their leaves shimmering in the late afternoon sun. Birds called to one another, and the river running nearby sang its own quiet song. Dust stirred by the horses' hooves and wagon wheels rose, coating Casey's new boots. She leaned down to brush it away. When the wagon clunked over a rock on the trail, she bounced again and almost lost her grip on the seat.

Chance slipped his right arm around her and moved her closer. "Wouldn't want to lose our cook."

They met the Hansons' group where North Star land met the Double Diamond. Chance parked the wagon in a wide, grassy pasture, near the Buffalo Fork River.

Casey remembered the spot from the day they went riding and stopped to see the Appaloosas. She jumped from the seat and opened the chuck wagon, pulling out the cooler and the basket of food to share between them. She looked around for Marianne, hoping the girl would help. She was nowhere to be seen.

"Here, let me do that." Chance grabbed the cooler. "You bring the rest. Morly set up a folding table, and the guys started the fire, so I'll get the steaks over there."

Casey tagged behind, appreciating the view of his broad shoulders and the hitch to his cowboy stride. He moved with such purpose, in spite of the bum knee, and watching him gave her a little thrill. The cool breeze off the river sifted through the willows and blew her hair. This would be a special night. She could feel it.

Before long, a campfire roared, and the aroma of sizzling steaks filled the soft valley twilight.

Later, sitting cross-legged on the ground, she balanced a tin plate on her lap and savored the potatoes roasted in the fire and the fresh bread she'd baked this morning. The cherry cobbler, a great complement, tasted sweet and tart on her tongue. The fresh open air and the company of people having a good time made the meal even more delicious, and she glanced at Chance as he approached to see if he was enjoying it. But as often happened, she found reading his thoughts almost impossible. She glanced around the group and caught sight of Kyle and Marianne.

Marianne offered Kyle a bite of the cobbler.

He laughed at something she said and playfully tugged at her long braid of dark hair.

She batted at his hand and pretended to scold.

Even from where she sat, Casey noticed the love light shining in the girl's eyes. At least, they were having a good time. "Those two seriously need to get together," she murmured.

"Quit being a mother hen." Chance handed her his plate and struggled to sit on the ground. "Kyle's a big boy. He can make his own decisions."

"I'm not so sure about that. I think he must be blind if he can't see how Marianne feels." Casey lifted her chin. "And I am not a mother hen."

"Then don't get your feathers ruffled." He took back his plate.

She sighed. "It's just that when two people are so well-suited and obviously belong together, it's a shame for them to stay apart."

Her gaze locked with his midnight-blue one, and the weight of what she'd just said played heavy on her heart. What about two people who were not well-suited, but who still felt undeniably attracted to each other? Did they belong together? A sweet, melting fire filled her every time Chance kissed her and held her in his arms. But Casey still feared whatever they had would never work out. "How did Justin act tonight?" She changed the subject. "Or weren't you up at the house at all?"

"I was there." Chance turned his attention to cutting a piece of steak on his plate.

"Was he moping around because Aunt Billie wasn't there?"

"Was he what?" He stuck the bite of meat in his mouth.

She rolled her eyes. "Your father. He didn't feel up to a ride, but was he upset about being left alone tonight?" The older man could be difficult. *Like father, like son.*

He chewed and swallowed. "Yeah, but he was worried about Billie. Said he might take a walk to her cabin later and make sure she's all right. Something about brewing up an herbal tea his mother used to make, a cure-all for any illness."

"I'm sure she'll love that. She hates being fussed over, even though she does it to everybody else."

"I suppose you think she and Justin ought to get

together, too." Chance stayed focused on his plate and attacked the rest of the steak.

Startled by his remark, Casey nevertheless didn't deny it. "It crossed my mind." She picked at her piece of bread and finally took a bite. What did Chance think of Justin and Billie getting romantic?

Jamie ran over and showed Casey his clean plate. "Can I have a cupcake now?"

"Sure. I'll get it for you, and you can help pass them around." She rose and turned to Chance. "Would you like a cupcake?"

"No, thanks." He got up and took his plate to the wagon.

Now what had ticked him off? Hard to tell with these McCord men. They were all a hardheaded bunch. Not much different from her own father and brother back home.

Refusing to let his brush-off spoil the evening, Casey headed to the wagon and the cupcakes. She might believe in eating healthy, but letting chocolate soothe a girl's soul had its merits

Chapter 14

Marianne and Casey packed up the chuckwagon and returned to the campfire. Someone suggested they sing a round of western songs, and Marianne started them on a familiar cowboy ballad. Their voices lifted above the crackle and pop of the fire and floated across the river to meld with the lonely, far-off song of a coyote.

After making sure Jamie was safely sitting with the kids, Casey looked around for Chance.

He sat apart from the group, leaning against the trunk of an aspen tree. The low brim of his hat hid his eyes, but their silent touch beckoned.

She curled beside him and rested in the curve of his shoulder, as if she had always belonged there. Sitting this way felt sweet and right. She loved the vibrant warmth of his skin pouring through the soft cotton shirt and the fresh scent that spoke of summer mountains, dusty hayfields, and sun-kissed pastures. She could call herself a fool for getting drawn in by all this, but for the moment, Casey just wanted to feel something beyond pain and sadness.

Darkness crept across the valley on cat feet, and the voice of the land hushed itself for the night. Smoke curled up from the campfire like ghostly gray fingers, drifting up to touch the million winking stars above them. A full moon rose and poured silver honey over the river, the grazing horses, and the faces of the folks gathered around the campfire.

Peering from beneath her lashes, Casey studied the face of the man beside her. As if carved in granite, immobile as the Tetons themselves, his expression betrayed no emotion. Yet beneath all that, a man existed who longed for and needed the same closeness she did. His whiskery chin skimmed her forehead, and she quivered.

Chance murmured something.

"What did you say?" Casey made the mistake of looking up. His dark sexy gaze sent a spark across her skin.

"That you smell good, kind of like…hmmm…"

"Summer Breeze?"

"Yeah, kind of like that."

He didn't have a clue what she was talking about, but the soft scent worked its magic.

In a second, he bent his head to kiss her.

Whatever was wrong between them just a while ago turned very right. Casey slipped her arm around him and relished the beating of his heart beneath the palm of her hand and the exquisite touch of his mouth on hers. She didn't care if they were wrong for each other; she just wanted the kiss to never end. In the shadows of the aspen, she gave up her heart and only wanted more.

The singing quieted for a moment.

"Hey, brother. You still out there?" Kyle spoke out.

Chance muttered a low growl and ended the kiss.

Startled, Casey pushed herself away and ran her fingers through her tangled hair. Had anyone seen them?

"Damn kid," he muttered and leaned away. "Yeah, whadda ya want?"

"How about giving us a little of that sad harmonica music you play so well? It's a good night for it, don't you think?"

Casey recognized Kyle's first friendly gesture toward Chance—an effort to close the yawning gap between the brothers?

Mrs. Richardson from Iowa clapped her hands together. "Oh yes, please do! We'd all love to hear you play."

Casey gave Chance a shove. "Go on. You better do it."

"I'd rather stay here with you." His voice dropped lower, and his sultry eyes shuttered closed as he leaned in for another kiss.

Casey stopped him with a hand over his mouth. "Just go. I need to check on Jamie."

He got up, and his knee popped, but he plucked the harmonica from his shirt pocket and limped away from the shadow of the aspen. "Sure, what would you folks like to hear?" In a moment, he made the little instrument sing, filling the valley with its brand of lonesome music.

Casey hugged her knees and rested her chin on them. Not ready to face the group yet, she let herself drift with the quivery strains of Chance playing the lilting, sweet song "Shenandoah." The haunting melody touched something deep inside her, and while the words might not be about a western river, the song spoke of the same winsome feelings this far-flung land evoked. Perhaps knowing she would soon leave Wyoming made this sudden ache swell in her heart.

When the last notes faded away to the stars, Casey made a furtive swipe at her eyes and swallowed the lump in her throat. If only she could remain here forever, listening to the music and the quiet rush of the river. If only…

"Play another one," someone said.

Chance obliged and drifted into the tune of an old cowboy song from over a hundred years ago.

In a clear, true voice, Marianne sang along.

When the song ended, the guests applauded, but a sudden gust of wind signaled the end of Chance's playing. The breeze that teased the campfire earlier suddenly picked up and sent tiny sparks whirling in a dizzy dance above them.

"Better get that fire out and head for home." Chance slipped the harmonica into his shirt pocket. "Could be a storm brewing." He doused the fire, then helped everyone saddle up. He paused a moment to rub the heel of his hand down his leg, while a grimace creased the corners of his mouth.

Casey watched, wanting to help but knowing if she showed any concern, he'd spurn it. She turned and called Jamie. "Do you want to ride in the wagon on the way back? It's been a long day. Aren't you too tired to ride Buckwheat?"

Jamie shook his head. "I'm not tired, and if I go in the wagon, who'll ride my pony?"

She tugged on his jacket while he protested. "Someone can lead your pony."

He pulled away, though his eyes drooped. "I'll be fine, Mom. Kyle said I could ride at the front of the line."

He wasn't ready to give in yet. "All right," Casey

relented. But where was Kyle? He'd been standing with the group a moment ago and now was nowhere around. Then she spied him strolling from the riverbank, one arm hooked around Marianne's waist. In the moonlight, a flush of happiness glowed on the young woman's face. She looked like she'd been thoroughly kissed.

As they wandered back to the group, Kyle pressed his lips to Marianne's hair.

Casey sighed. Perhaps their relationship would work out. Chilling in the night air, she slipped on her quilted vest and turned back to Jamie, but he'd already clambered astride the pony. "I still think you should ride with—"

"It's okay, Ms. Casey. I'll keep an eye on the boy," Roy called out.

Casey waved and gave him a small smile. Roy was always around when she needed him.

He nodded and rode off with Jamie and Buckwheat.

Casey watched the wrangler guide Jamie to the head of the line. Did the McCords recognize Roy's unwavering loyalty to the North Star?

The groups separated, waving and calling good-byes. Once more, the wagon brought up the rear.

Sitting beside Chance this time, Casey shoved her hands into the pockets of the vest and hunched her shoulders against the night's cool breeze. Since putting the harmonica away, he'd been silent again. Was he embarrassed playing in front of all those people? He had a way of doing something and then feeling self-conscious, as if he hated the attention. But seriously, hadn't he drawn attention as a bronc rider? What was different now? "We all enjoyed the songs you played."

She could still hear those soft quivery notes and tried to hold back a shiver, but it rippled through her.

"Here, scoot over." Chance put his right arm around her and drew her close.

Once more, Casey rested her head in the hollow above his chest.

He rubbed his hand up and down her arm.

The friction against the chambray quickly warmed her.

"I'll bet you've got cold feet, too." He chuckled softly. "Do you wear fuzzy socks to bed?"

Matt often teased her about her fuzzy socks, and the thought of another man knowing things about her that only he knew made for an awkward moment. But Chance understood things intuitively, and with him this close again, she didn't want distance rising between them. Just for tonight, she wanted to treasure this hour alone. "Only in the winter."

Chance let the horses pick their own pace. The Belgians moved slowly and lagged behind the others.

The wagon swayed in slow motion, lulling Casey and easing away her doubts.

"Did you have a good time?"

His breath stirred the hair at her temple. "Mm hm. I think everybody did. But tell me something. Did you really learn to play the harmonica from a barrel man?"

"Yep. Hank and I got to be pretty good buddies. We spent a lot of nights sitting up and shooting the bull. I was nothing but a dumb green kid when I first went down the road. In a way, Hank took the place of Sam Murphy in my life."

"You must have thought a lot of him. Where is Hank now?"

"He's got a little spread in Colorado. He left the rodeo some years ago, while he was still in one piece, and married a rodeo gal. Laverne is a three-time barrel-racing champ." He hesitated and shifted his left hand over the harness lines. "Hank put me up after I blew out my knee last year. He and Laverne treated me well. If not for them, I'd be in worse shape. They were more like family than my own."

At the sound of an owl hooting, she looked up and marveled at how many stars had popped out since they left the cookout. Was there any sky as wide as Wyoming's? She could gaze at it all night and not talk, but a nagging question dwelled in her mind. "Chance, why didn't you let your family know what happened? Did you think they wouldn't care?" Since they had grown closer, Casey felt she had the right to ask, but she heard a low rumble in his chest.

"Humph. Why should they? They hadn't heard from me in five years. You think I'm going to call and say, hey, I got thrown off a bucking horse one too many times and now I need your help?"

"Maybe if you had, you wouldn't have this huge rift." He kept his arm around her, but Casey felt him withdraw. She sat upright. He'd set his mouth in a firm line, and even in the darkness, his eyes burned with a stormy hue. He might keep things secret, but this time, she wouldn't let it happen. This time, she would know why Chance held himself apart. She touched his whiskery cheek and slid her hand over his clenched jaw, forcing him to face her. "Don't do that to me, cowboy. Don't you dare pull down that mask and pretend you're so almighty tough. Something's been bothering you all night, and I want to know what it is."

Chance gave a tug on the harness lines, and the horses stopped. His gaze locked with hers in a sudden battle of wills. "Wow, the lady can be feisty," he drawled.

"Maybe not feisty enough, but I'm learning, Chance. You are quite a good teacher. You are also an exasperating man, and if you think you can tease your way out of this, think again. If the injury is bothering you, maybe you ought to see another doctor. Sometimes, things don't heal the way they should and—"

"What's bothering me tonight, Casey Girard, doesn't have a damn thing to do with my knee."

His low and husky voice stopped her tirade. She stared.

Chance's gaze softened, but his eyes burned with dark fire. "It's a whole lot more than that, and most of what's bothering me is you. If you don't know by now how bad I want you, want us, to be together, then maybe I should just spell it. I. Want. You. Now. Right here. Or anywhere. I want to make love to you, and it's driving me crazy." His jaw worked back and forth.

Her pulse fluttered, and she swallowed hard. His desire didn't shock her. From their first kiss, she'd known how he felt, but the blatant admission bounced around inside her like a bunch of well-aimed darts. Any second, one of them would find her heart and burst it wide open. She tried to speak, but nothing came out.

His chest rose and fell in a rapid rhythm. "But if you want to know another truth, I'll tell you. Yes, the injuries I got last year still hurt like hell, but that's a pain I can live with. It's other things I can't. Things from the past that I can't forgive or forget, or get past, no matter how hard I've tried. And it's the pain from them that will follow me all the rest of my life."

A few weeks ago, even a few days, Casey would have thought her ache was just empathy for another person in pain, but now, she recognized the feeling. Love. Plain and simple. Only in this case, not so simple. Chance would never be an easy man to love. Yet, she loved him. No denying it. "Then let's talk about it. Tell me about those things from the past. I'm a good listener." She placed her hand on his chest. "Life hurt me, too, and there isn't anything you can say that I won't understand." The cool breeze lifted strands of her hair and blew them across her upturned face.

With a soft groan, Chance dropped the lines and tangled his hands in her hair. He pulled her close. "The trouble is"—he hovered his mouth just inches from hers—"with all those western stars above us, the last thing I want to do right now is talk."

He closed the small distance between them and took possession of her lips with the force of a mountain storm. There was no gentle coaxing this time, nor teasing first tastes. He'd kissed her before, and now their kisses needed to say more. He pulled Casey close and wrapped his arms around her.

His heartbeat went wild beneath her hands, and control slipped away behind a fast-falling curtain of desire. No other time existed but this, no other man but the one who held her. All else that ever happened in her life drifted far away, and Casey knew only Chance…and the endless purple mountains with their pink-hued sky…and the keening winds that roared down from the jagged peaks and ripped across the valley…and the sun that shone like warm sweet honey on the days…and the moon that flowed in silver rivers across the night. Like a mountain flower reawakening beneath the touch of the sun, Casey parted her lips, and the song of love sang in her heart while a fierce longing to be one with Chance consumed all rational thought.

And then he set her away, and the transition from being held in his arms to sitting alone threw her off balance. She gripped the wooden seat again to keep from falling over the side.

Chance turned and fumbled for his hat that had fallen at their feet. He crushed it between his hands before jamming it on his head and leaping to the ground. "I'm sorry. I shouldn't…let this happen."

Casey opened her mouth to absolve him from all the blame.

With a sweep of his hand, he cut her off. "No, please don't give me any of that patient understanding of yours. I can't handle it right now."

Sliced to the quick, Casey bit her still-sensitive lip. Holding onto whatever dignity she could, she stared off into the darkness. Across the valley drifted the soft lowing of cattle, the muted cry of a night bird, and the far-off yip of a coyote. Sounds that might have soothed her moments ago now did nothing to assuage the pain tearing at her heart.

"I won't deny what I feel for you, Casey. It's something I thought I'd never feel again in my life. I want you, but I don't know if it's enough to make me forget what went before."

"Does it matter what went before? I hurt, too." Tears blurred her eyes. "But maybe we can learn from each other how to live with that kind of pain."

"I wish I could believe that." Chance braced his

shoulders and stepped back from the wagon. He jutted his chin toward the others, who moved farther along the trail. "You go ahead. Mac and Red know their way home. You'll be all right." A determined look crossed his features.

Anger flared and replaced Casey's tears. "Gee, thanks for the consideration. I guess what they say about cowboys is true. They will only break your heart."

He rubbed a hand down his face and stared off behind them. "Yeah, maybe you're right."

"And what about you?" Casey picked up the harness lines, a trickle of unease niggling at her. "What are you going to do?" Would he just disappear into the night?

"I'll be fine." He jerked his head toward the trail. "And anyway, here's Roy."

The wrangler halted his horse close by. "What's up? Problem with the wagon?" He flicked his glance between them.

Chance tugged his hat brim down and moved farther away from the trail. "No problem, just…make sure Casey gets back all right, will you?"

She wanted to fling words that would hurt him the way he'd hurt her, but she gathered the lines in her trembling hands. They had shared some fiery, passionate kisses but now were miles apart. She had nothing more to say.

"Sure, Chance." Roy reined his horse closer. "Do you want me to drive, Ms. Casey?"

She lifted her chin. "No, I can manage. But if you'd ride alongside, I'd appreciate it." As they drew away, a sense of finality replaced anything else Casey felt for Chance. Would he always handle a problem this way—by bowing out and running away? That possibility settled like a cold rain. If the ghosts of his past were just too many for him to overcome, then she wouldn't lose any more of her heart than she already had. To have fallen in love with him was her folly, but to let that love grow if he couldn't return it would be the most foolish thing of all.

She reminded herself of that all the way home and long after she put Jamie to bed and wrapped herself in a blanket to curl up by the bedroom window. Somehow, the realization didn't sink in, and she still wondered if Chance would make it home.

****

Watching the wagon pull away, Chance struggled to control the flood of emotions that threatened to consume him. If only he could explain to Casey, make her understand, that when that familiar pain drove its fiery poker through him, he felt divided in two. Part of him wanted to move forward in life, but part clung stubbornly to the past. Tonight, they were more at war with each other than ever, and until he found some middle ground, he couldn't ask Casey to share his life.

The walk home on foot would take a while, and he might encounter anything, but walking alone in the night had its advantages. Without the blinding light of day, a man could pretend ugly truths didn't exist, and darkness provided its own solace. Before he'd gone far, some of the pain eased away, but as always, it left him raw inside. He'd hoped Casey could take away the rawness and heal the still-open wound, but as much as he wanted to believe they could have a future together, he had to take this walk alone. He couldn't expect

Casey, or anyone else, to fix him.

Reminded of other unhealed wounds, he gritted his teeth as he felt his knee wrench, nearly landing him in the dust. Stifling a groan, he limped off the trail. A nearby rock provided a good place to sit and think about why he hadn't had that second surgery. Hank and Laverne were more than willing to let him stay on, but being obliged to folks, even good friends, went against his nature. He could still hear Hank's parting words echoing in his brain. "Don't be a fool, man. You don't listen to the doc, you're gonna end up not walking at all. Is that what you want?"

Chance had been packing to leave the Colorado ranch, stuffing his few belongings into a duffel bag. "I'll be okay. You've done enough for me, and I don't want to overstay my welcome."

"You know that's crazy," the outspoken Laverne said. "We don't care how long you stay, Chance. You're not healed yet, and going on down the road before you are is a bad idea."

He paused and took in the concern on their kind faces. How could he explain? The pain of broken body parts was nothing compared to the pain of a broken heart. If he could survive that, he could survive anything. "I appreciate everything you two have done for me, but it's time to go. There are things I need to settle, and soon, before it's too late." Lying in a hospital bed after this last fall had given him way too much time to think. Running away had solved nothing. The loss would always be with him, but maybe going back would somehow put pain in its place.

Laverne sighed and shook her head. "Can't we change your mind?"

He ignored her bewildered tone and zipped up the duffel. "Nope. My mind's made up."

"Then, at least, stay for dinner and leave in the morning." The redhead gave her best cajoling smile. "I made your favorite special chocolate pie with a ton of whipped cream."

The rodeo queen could be persuasive. Her offer made him remember his own family hadn't been that upset to see him go. In fact, he was pretty sure Justin and Kyle were relieved—both times. "You sure know how to tempt a man, Laverne. I'll take you up on that offer. Might be a long time before I hear one that good again."

Before he left in the morning, Chance felt Hank's hand on his shoulder and heard his parting words.

"You do what you gotta do, but if you need us, we're here. Remember that."

Chance shook his best friend's hand. Hank understood what drove him. He'd seen the photograph.

Now, months later, on a star-filled night in Wyoming, Chance slipped the photograph from his pocket and traced the image with his fingers. The features of that sweet face would remain forever in his heart. Some days, the memories faded; maybe the real reason he returned to the North Star. Losing the memories would be almost as devastating as losing the child, and even though they were painful, he wanted to keep the memories alive. The past five years, pain had been his constant companion, but he'd learned some things one could never lay to rest. A man just had to live with them the best way he could and find a different path to follow.

A sound drew his attention away from the

photograph.

A big furry dog landed in his lap and about knocked him off the rock. Leave it to the old dog to find him.

Mariah lapped his face with her joyful tongue.

"Hey, what's this? Did you decide to come after me?" He ruffled her floppy ears.

She rested her head on his arm. After a moment, Mariah ran back to the trail. She stopped there and whined.

"Okay, I get the message." Chance pocketed the photograph and got to his feet. He hobbled toward Mariah and put a hand on her sturdy neck. "Afraid I need some help getting home, old girl."

Mariah stayed at his side as beneath the star-filled sky, they made their way back to the bunkhouse.

For the next hour, he let the old dog guide him, but he had to stop every few minutes and rest, so the damn knee didn't buckle. The entire time, a million regrets filled his head for the way he'd treated Casey. Would she even speak to him after the things he'd said? He wouldn't blame her if she totally ignored him, but the thought of her leaving ripped a hole through his gut. How could he make it up to her? How could he fix what might be irreparably broken?

Chapter 15

July fell away and drifted into August. The dry weather held, and the hay-cutting time passed. Irrigating began again, a job that required someone to move the dams that channeled the water from the canals to the ditches that zigzagged through the pastures and hayfields.

"Chance took on the job," Billie told Casey one morning. "He'll drive the pickup out to the dams and haul them out of the ditches to place in the next spot. Have to say one thing about him. He hasn't shirked his share of work this summer."

Casey cracked eggs into a bowl and beat them harder than necessary. She and Chance had talked little since that night he'd walked home alone. She'd lain awake for a few restless nights, remembering all the things he'd said and how he'd kissed her...and how she'd kissed him back...before he set her aside like she meant nothing.

Hearing his name mentioned now needled like a thousand pinpricks. "He thinks he needs to prove himself after being gone so long." She dumped salt and pepper into the eggs. "To his own family."

Billie turned the coffeemaker on. "That's the way it works with the men here, Casey. They always feel the need to prove something, if not to themselves, then to somebody else. You better get used to it if you're going to—"

"I'm not." She beat the eggs harder and tossed the fork into the sink. "Jamie and I are heading back to Michigan before the end of the month."

Billie only nodded

When Jamie found out Chance was driving the truck to the hayfield, he begged to tag along.

Reluctantly, Casey let him go but struggled with her decision. She shouldn't have let him spend so much time with Chance this summer, but Jamie needed the attention and companionship of a man. He'd thrived and grown at least two inches under Chance's watchful eye, and she didn't have the heart to cut the friendship short, even if her own relationship with Chance was over.

August proved the busiest time with the guest ranch. She and Billie worked from early morning until late evening, playing hostess for the people spending their end of summer at the North Star. By ten o'clock at night, she was too tired to do anything but fall into bed, but she didn't mind. Work kept her from thinking about Chance and lying awake, listening for the soft harmonica music. The few times a song drifted through the night brought back the memory of the last time he'd kissed her. The last time. She'd made up her mind. She treated him pleasantly for Jamie's sake, but putting distance between herself and Chance was simple reasoning on her part and perfect logic. If she didn't allow herself to feel anything more than she already did, leaving wouldn't hurt so much.

They could go home sooner than the last week in August, but she hated leaving Billie with so much work. Of course, Billie had coped before, but she'd had

Sam to keep her going. Casey suspected Billie dreaded the day she was left alone in her little cabin.

Justin hatched the idea that put an enjoyable spark in the last long days of summer but also put another demand on Casey's time. "I think it's an excellent idea." He leaned back in his swivel leather chair. His silver-blue eyes twinkled. "What do you think, Casey?"

She'd slipped into his study to check on the progress of the book, and he'd cajoled her into keeping him company for a while. Just long enough for him to launch his latest scheme—giving campfire talks to the ranch guests about the part the McCord family had played in settling the valley.

"I know you've got more than enough work to do, what with helping Billie and all, but I'm sure the guests would much rather listen to a pretty woman than an old goat like me."

"Oh, I don't know about that." Perched on the arm of the nearby easy chair, Casey sent him a teasing smile. "You're a darn handsome cowboy. I'm sure you'd have all the ladies coming around. Maybe even some wealthy widow who might make Billie jealous."

"Humph," Justin grunted. He shoved his hands into his jeans pockets and got up to pace around the room. "That woman is another story all together. I've known her for over forty years, since she first came here with Sam. But I'll be damned if I can figure her out. Don't know how Sam stood it as many years as he did. She was forever picking on that poor man."

"He loved it, and so do you. In fact, I think you and Billie should give the campfire talks. You might even, you know, discover a little romance."

Justin wheeled around and lifted one shaggy brow.

"Billie and me?"

Casey raised her hands in a nonchalant shrug. "Sure, why not? Isn't love sweeter the second time around?"

Beneath the curve of his mustache, Justin pursed his mouth into a frown. "To tell the truth, I've thought of it. It might seem foolish for two old codgers like us, but even if she's prickly, I care for Billie. When she's not around needling me about one thing or another, I miss her."

"Then tell her! I mean, why wait any longer?"

Justin nodded slowly. He raised an eyebrow. "Billie tells me it's been nearly three years since you lost your husband. Isn't it time for you to do something about that?"

Casey clasped her hands and stared at them. "I...haven't thought much about it." Not entirely true, but she would never admit it to Justin.

"Your boy needs a father."

"We do just fine by ourselves." Not quite true either, though she'd done her best to be both mother and father to Jamie. "Matt was a wonderful father. I'm not sure Jamie needs anyone else."

"Hmmm, yes, so does that mean you're holding him up as an ideal?"

Justin's quiet, probing question struck a sensitive chord. Perhaps she was doing exactly that. Holding Matt up as the model for which every other man fell short...including Chance. "It's going to be hard to find someone as special as Matt." They'd had their problems, but Matthew Girard had been her hero...and still was.

"I suppose it will, especially since you've built him

into such a paragon of virtue. I suspect your Matthew was as human as the rest of us, with just as many faults and weaknesses. Not too many of us are perfect."

Her dashing pilot husband hadn't been perfect, but she'd loved him. Tears suddenly burned Casey's eyes. She didn't want to embarrass herself and struggled to hold them back.

Justin stood in front of her and put a hand under her chin. He tipped her face and gave her a reassuring smile. "You know, I've become fond of you, Casey, and I'd never intend to hurt you. I know what it's like losing someone with whom you were so close. It's like that person is another part of you. It's hard to love again."

She didn't bother to hide the tears slipping down her cheeks. Memories of Matt still hurt, though time had worked its healing power and given her some peace where his loss was concerned. But now there was Chance, who without warning had put his own brand on her heart.

"Making you cry is not what I had in mind today." Justin gave Casey's damp cheek a pat and offered his own clean white handkerchief. "Asking you to give a few little evening talks about the history of my ranch is. Will you do it, Casey? I think it's something our guests would enjoy. Maybe eventually we'd keep it as a regular feature."

She dabbed her eyes and blew her nose. "Of course, I'll do it. You know I will, but promise me you'll back me up. After all, you are the cowboy."

He shook his snowy head and gave a loud guffaw. "Go on with you, now. I've got work to do here. You come back tonight, and we'll get this program figured out." Justin settled himself behind the mahogany desk. "I realize neither of my sons is perfect. They both take after me in all the worst ways, but Chance has always been the one who needed something more than we could give him. I like to think you might be who he needs, Casey. He might never measure up to your Matthew, but he's a good man. You could do a whole lot worse than him."

For the rest of the day, she mulled Justin's words over in her head. What he'd said surprised her. Father and son were always arguing about something, and his comments were the opposite of what Marianne had told her. *He's the kind who never settles down. They always have an itch to move on. He'll only hurt you.* How could they be talking about the same man?

The two opposing arguments whirled around in her mind until she had a headache and was more confused than ever. She wanted to believe Chance was a good man. Hadn't he already shown her that many times? And he wanted her. He'd said so. But did want equal love? Neither had spoken that word. Perhaps he didn't want to be tied down, no matter what he might feel. Perhaps he still fostered notions of one day leaving the North Star again. She could never deal with that. How could she risk loving a man who might one day just up and leave with little regard for his family? After what they'd been through, it wouldn't be fair to either her or Jamie. Losing Matt was something beyond her control. Losing Chance, now she loved him, would hurt in a far different way. How would she ever deal with the situation?

Chapter 16

A few days later, the campfire talk drew a crowd. Eager to learn what life was like on the ranch over a hundred years ago, the guests flocked to the temporary circle of camp chairs Casey set up around the fire ring, just beyond the corrals. Nights turned even cooler now in August, and the crackling fire lent warmth and a friendly atmosphere to the gathering.

The first night, Casey told them about Garett and Martha McCord, who had settled in the valley between the mountains, battled wild rivers, bitter blizzards, and the competition of ranchers already established and built a homestead of their own. That homestead would become the North Star Ranch. She even engaged the kids in the audience with the story of "Drifter Pete," a longhorn who helped establish the North Star's first herd. She planned the program much like the story hours she ran at her library, and answering their questions made the story come alive. Having read Martha McCord's journal, she needed little prompting from Justin.

He sat back and listened while Casey related the North Star's legacy, a wide smile on his craggy face.

The second night, she talked about the history of the state. "John Colter was the first European known to travel to what we call Wyoming in about 1807. He saw the Tetons, and when he told people about the wonders here and in Yellowstone, they laughed and called him a liar. Then the trappers came and soon the pioneers. Women faced a lot of hardships, but they played a big part in the settling of this state. Wyoming saw many firsts for women. In 1870, the district court in Laramie seated the first woman on a jury. Jackson was the first town governed by women and had a lady sheriff. Wyoming was the first state to give women the right to vote, and its nickname is the Equality State."

The women in her audience all cheered.

"But it's the Cowboy State, too, because there's a cowboy on a bucking horse on the license plate," one of the kids piped up.

"You're right, and his name was Steamboat," Casey added. "He's a symbol you'll see everywhere here." She'd even noticed a statue of the cowboy and bronco at the airport where she and Jamie flew in. "But that's a story for another night."

The fire had burned down, and the younger kids were nodding off.

She invited them all back the following evening to hear more about the bucking bronco and make s'mores.

"I think we could use you around here all the time." Justin gave her a hug. "What would it take to convince you to stay?"

A teasing glint shone in his silver-blue eyes, but she suspected Justin was serious and would love for her to live at the North Star permanently. Maybe he hoped it would make Chance stay, but as much as she loved it here, Chance staying wasn't a given. He'd left twice before. Smiling, she brushed off his question without answering and turned to marshal her son off to bed.

"Do I hafta?" Jamie hid a yawn behind a grubby

hand.

"Yes, you hafta." Casey put an arm around his shoulders and steered him toward the cabin.

Halfway down the path, Chance caught up and fell in step beside them.

Casey's heart tripped over itself, but she kept walking. Why did she have to fall for someone like him? A man who was as unpredictable as the sudden storms that blew up over the Tetons and disappeared just as quickly. She quickened her pace.

Jamie hurried alongside but glanced up at Chance. "Did you hear my mom tonight?"

Chance's stride easily matched hers. "I did, and she sounded pretty good."

"Mr. McCord wants her to stay here. And I think we should. Then you and me could go fishing. We didn't get to do that. Wouldn't you like to stay, Mom?" He turned his gaze to Casey.

She kept walking, but the touch of another, darker gaze burned into her, leaving her a little breathless. She tried to ignore Chance. "It's not a matter of if I want to, Jamie." Casey attempted to explain. "I have a job, and all our family is in Michigan. Wouldn't you miss Grandma and Grandpa? And your cousins?"

"Sure, I guess so, but we don't see them that much. And I don't get to ride horses at home. I'll miss Buckwheat."

The sad note in Jamie's voice tugged at Casey. She stopped on the path and put her hands on his narrow shoulders. "I'm sure you will. Maybe we'll come back to Wyoming for a visit someday."

Jamie shrugged her hands away and remained silent the rest of the way to the cabin. "I can put myself to bed." He opened the door and went inside alone.

She would have followed him, anyway.

Chance held her back with a light hand on her arm. "Let the boy go for now. Sometimes, even kids need to be by themselves. Billie's there if he needs anything." He patted her shoulder.

Casey peered in the front window, where a soft light glowed.

Billie sat in her favorite easy chair, reading glasses propped on her nose. A book lay open on her lap. She glanced up when the boy entered alone and headed straight for the bedroom.

Jamie's sudden streak of independence stabbed at Casey. Parenting had its challenging moments, and she wasn't nearly ready for Jamie pulling away. She sank onto the top porch step. "Maybe this wasn't such a good idea, after all."

"What wasn't?" Chance eased down beside her and stretched out his legs. He took off his hat, set it on the step, and rubbed at his knee with the heel of one hand.

"Coming out here for the summer. I hoped it would be good for Jamie and me to get away for a while. I thought it would help him forget the sad memories, but now, I'm not so sure I did the right thing. Maybe my mother's right, and I'm just making too many wrong decisions." She covered her face with her hands.

"Remember what I told you about that."

"Yes, but there are a lot of books on childrearing, and I've read many, but I still often wonder if what I'm doing is the best thing." If only Matt were alive to share these problems. But then, if he were alive, she would never have come to Wyoming.

Chance leaned a little closer. "Casey-honey, you

need to quit being so hard on yourself. You're a terrific mom, but you can't expect to shield Jamie from every disappointment in life. He's gotta learn to deal with them the same as anybody else."

Casey dropped her hands from her face and gazed out at the twilight that lingered just past the pine grove. Shadows peeked through the branches and snuck along the ground. "I suppose you're right, but isn't it only natural for a mother to protect her child and keep him from being hurt? The thing is, now I feel like I've heaped more hurt on Jamie by bringing him here. Taking him away seems almost cruel."

Chance put an arm around Casey.

The affectionate gesture bore no passion, and she leaned against him. They sat together for a while, listening to the soft whickering of the horses and the familiar, far-off song of a coyote. Another peaceful, sage-scented western night settled down on them. She would miss nights like this.

"There is one way you could keep Jamie from being hurt," he murmured close to her ear.

"What's that?" Casey met his steady gaze.

He searched her face intently. "Stay on here. Work for Justin. It would make the old man happy."

Would it make you happy? Do you want me to stay? "I have a home, and I'm going back to it soon."

A shadow stole over his face. "To what? A life alone in an apartment?"

She shrugged. "To my job and raising my son." What did he think she would do?

Chance half-laughed. "You can do that here. The way you talked to those people tonight, Justin would love for you to conduct a program like that all summer.

179

You could put your love of history to good use."

She touched a pearl snap on the front of his shirt, feeling the heat of his skin through the soft cotton. "Yes, but summer is almost over."

"We have a library in town. You could work there, and you could help Justin with his book. It's a healthy atmosphere for a growing boy. This western land goes far in shaping a man. Just look at Kyle and me." A teasing light shone in his midnight-blue eyes. He brushed a finger across her cheek. "You could have a good life here, Casey. You and Jamie both."

Casey sensed a change. "Would it matter to you if we stayed?" She had to know if what Chance felt went beyond just wanting.

He drew her closer and cupped a hand along her face. "It would matter very much if you stayed." He leaned in and kissed her.

Her lips trembled beneath his, and a single tear trickled down her cheek.

Chance broke off the kiss. "Hey, now what is this? Why is it I always make you cry? Is it something about the way I kiss?"

Casey put her arms around his neck and buried her face against him. "I've been crying a lot. I don't know why."

He held her and stroked her back until the crying jag subsided. "Maybe it's because you're kissing a cowboy with a bum knee and a banged-up body. I know I'm no prize."

"No, of course, it's not that." Casey lifted her head and pushed her hair away from her face. "I don't care how banged up you are. It's just…I don't understand. You draw me close, only to push me away. If you care about me, why do you do that?"

He sighed heavily and took his arms from around her. Folding both her hands in his, he held them close. "Because all summer, I've been fighting myself. I knew I was falling for you before we went on that ride to the Double Diamond, and I didn't want that to happen."

She sniffed. "But why?" Maybe he didn't want the responsibility of a family, because he didn't want anyone tying him down.

"Why?" His dark gaze searched hers. "I can never be the man you need or the kind you deserve. I've led a pretty self-centered life. I didn't want anyone to count on me for anything. But that hasn't kept me from learning to care about you. And I do care, Casey. More than I thought I could ever care about someone again."

Maybe that should have been all Casey needed to hear, but somehow, his answer wasn't enough. She read a wealth of sadness in his dark eyes, but doubt still dwelled in her heart that if she stayed, she would only end up getting hurt. Because he'd still not said the word love.

He dipped his head down and looked her in the face. "Am I foolish to think you could accept me for the man I am?"

Casey turned her face away. "Not foolish at all, but…I'm afraid."

He pulled back. "Of me?"

"Of you leaving again. You say you care about me, but would that stop you from leaving if the urge hit you? If you wanted to go back on the rodeo circuit? I couldn't put myself or Jamie through that." She saw a stunned look come over his face.

He let go of her hands. "Do you honestly think I

would do that to you and Jamie?"

Casey lifted her tear-filled gaze. "I don't know. Would you? If you're so unsure of being the man you think I need, how can I be sure you wouldn't just up and leave one day? You left your home before with no consideration for your family. How do I know you wouldn't do it again?"

Chance picked up his hat and ran his fingers around the inside of the brim. The corners of his mouth tugged down. "I guess you don't. But know this, Casey. I would never do anything to hurt you or that little boy. My running days are over. I just wish you could believe that." He left her then, heading along the path until he disappeared behind the tall pine trees.

She watched him go, seeing the end of their relationship before it had ever begun. Casey stood and gathered her thoughts. In the days and weeks ahead, would she blame herself for letting Chance go? *Probably.* Would she regret her decision not to stay? *For sure.* But whether she stayed here or went home, either way she'd have a broken heart.

Inside the cabin, Billie had tucked Jamie into bed and settled back in her chair. She took one look at Casey and motioned for her to sit. "Things aren't going so well for you and Chance, are they? I should've warned you at the beginning he's not an easy man to love, but I think even then it would've been too late. You were already half-hooked when you gave him that ride to the ranch."

Kicking off her shoes, Casey slumped in Sam's old chair and tucked her legs under her. "I hate to say it, Aunt Billie, but I think you're right."

Even on that day nearly two months ago, when

she'd first met Chance in the café, she'd sensed an electric tension between them. A powerful awareness of each other as a man and a woman had hummed in the air. If only she'd taken that moment as a warning and kept her distance. But second-guessing did little good now. She had fallen in love with Chance and would have to deal with all the pain of that folly.

"So, what's the problem?" Billie gently prodded. "I'm willing to say the man's crazy about you. Jamie certainly wouldn't mind staying here. No job can be so important that you wouldn't put your personal life first. What's holding you two apart?"

How could she explain? Casey rested her head on the back of the chair and fought off another bout of tears. "I can't help feeling that, even if we stay, he might one day decide he wants to leave the ranch again. He says his running days are over, and I want to believe him, but…"

Billie studied her for a long moment, then she nodded. "It's for pretty sure Chance hasn't told you, and nobody else around here or in the valley can talk about it. But I think it's time you heard the whole story of why he left the North Star the second time. If you love him, you *need* to know." Billie set her book aside and scooted to the edge of her chair. She clasped her sturdy hands together.

Casey wound her hair into a knot and steadied herself. Did she want to hear this? But perhaps by knowing his past, she would understand the man Chance was now. "What happened, Aunt Billie?"

Billie's brown eyes darkened. A small smile lifted the corners of her mouth. "Angela is what happened. Angela Harris, a sweet, pretty girl from down around

Pinedale. She was working at a restaurant in Cody, waiting tables for the summer to help pay for college. She went to the rodeo one night with some friends. Chance was named best all-around cowboy and was the hero of the day. Angie said she fell head over heels the minute she saw him. Some friends introduced them, and he was just as struck. It's enough to say she never returned to college. They were married a few weeks later, but her parents weren't at all pleased. They even came here, begging Justin to help them break it up between Chance and Angie."

Stunned by this revelation, Casey sat straighter in the easy chair. "Did he?"

Billie frowned and shook her head. "Justin had long ago stopped trying to run his older son's life. From what Chance told me later, he and Angie were doing fine, and she didn't even mind the constant moving around from one rodeo to another. They had themselves a little trailer, and it was like one long honeymoon…until she got pregnant. I guess that scared her, and she insisted they settle down. The idea of impending fatherhood knocked some sense into Chance. He brought Angie home to the North Star. Scottie was born six months later."

Chance had a wife and son. The knowledge gave her a sickening jolt and sparked a flood of questions. Was he hiding from that? What had happened to them? Were he and Angela estranged? Divorced?

Billie took off her glasses. "Chance was only twenty-three, but he made a real effort to quit the circuit and be a good husband and father. He took to learning the ranch business, and for a time, he and Justin finally got along. They built a grudging respect between them, and Justin loved his grandson dearly. He and Chance took that boy everywhere. Had him up on Buckwheat before he could even walk." Billie rubbed her eyes and cleared her throat. "Trouble was Kyle felt left out in the cold. He'd been the favored son all this time and grew up hearing Chance called the black sheep and the prodigal son. Kyle couldn't accept his brother being treated as a welcome member of the family."

Finding out Chance had once been married was like a light switching on in the dark. Maybe this explained a lot about his character and the ghosts he talked about in his past. "But what about Angela? How did this all affect her? Living amidst all that conflict couldn't have been easy."

Billie sat back in her chair again. "She couldn't handle it. Living here got to be too much for her. She grew up on a ranch, but the North Star is more isolated. She didn't like being so far from her friends and her own family, who still didn't like Chance, even after the baby came."

"I can imagine the hardship, but she had Chance and her son. That didn't make her happy?"

"Living out here is difficult, even for the toughest folks. Angie was a sweet girl. She just couldn't cope. She was too fragile, emotionally and physically, and she felt useless and unable to fit in. You want to know the saddest part? Chance didn't seem to notice. He was too busy trying to please his father, while working the ranch and all. He left Angie too much on her own. He paid a lot of attention to his son, but he and Angie grew distant. One day, she just left. She took Scottie, and she left the North Star." Billie hesitated going on.

Casey knew she hadn't heard the end of the story.

She didn't think Angie's leaving was the real reason Chance left the ranch and went back to the rodeo life. "What happened then?"

Billie breathed a shaky sigh. "Chance and Justin were away from the ranch the day she left. Chance didn't even know she was gone 'til he got home that night. Sam and I were gone, too. We didn't know what had happened 'til they came to tell us."

"Who came?" She held her breath, afraid to know the answer.

Billie pressed her lips together in a thin line. "Wyoming Highway Patrol." She leaned over and reached into the drawer of the end table beside her chair, taking out the envelope, and opening it to where a newspaper clipping lay folded inside. Silently, she withdrew the clipping and handed it to Casey.

An icy chill crept over her as she lifted the clipping. The headline jumped out, and a nauseating fear gripped her heart.

ICE SLICK ROADS CLAIM TWO LIVES

Prominent rancher's wife and son victims of freak storm.

Casey's pulse quickened, but she made herself read on.

Angela McCord of the North Star Ranch was killed late Friday afternoon, along with her five-year-old son Scottie, when the car she was driving slid across the ice-covered highway near Pinedale and careened into a jackknifed semi-trailer. Highway Patrol, who investigated the accident, said that Mrs. McCord and her young son were heading southeast when she lost control of her vehicle on icy roads.

Freezing rain had been falling for about an hour

when the mishap occurred. Another passenger in the car, Kyle McCord, had minor injuries. The driver of the semi sustained numerous injuries.

She didn't need to read more. Never in a million years had she suspected such a tragedy shadowed Chance's past. She bit her bottom lip, unable to imagine the pain of losing not only his wife but his child. She couldn't fathom the depth of the grief. "This is what he's running from. The loss must have been terrible for Chance. For the whole family."

"It was hard. It still is." Billie took the newspaper clipping from Casey and stared at it for a long moment. "Kyle's being with her made it even worse. To this day, Chance believes his brother was running away with his wife."

This didn't fit the Kyle Casey knew. "Is that true? I mean, Kyle would have been younger than Angie, right?"

"Only by a few years." Billie slipped the clipping into the envelope and settled back in her chair. "I used to see Angie and Kyle heading out past the corrals after supper. She seemed so happy when she was with him. I wondered if she didn't marry the wrong brother."

"But do you really think…"

Billie shrugged. "I guess that's something only Kyle knows for sure. After Chance left the ranch again, Kyle never spoke about Angie or his brother. And it's taken him all this time to even so much as look at another woman. It's good to see him with Marianne. Maybe some real healing can finally get started." She returned the envelope to the drawer and got up from her chair while rubbing her back. "I'm heading off to bed now. Turn off the lights when you turn in."

Casey nodded but stayed curled up in the chair, thinking about what she had just learned. Something Chance had said this evening played back in her mind—that he cared for her more than he thought he could care for anyone again. She should have realized that a deep hurt dwelled inside of Chance. Just coming back to the North Star must have been so painful for him—seeing the place where his son had been a baby, had followed him around, and ridden Buckwheat. Surprising he'd even come back at all. Maybe for Kyle the healing had begun, but for Chance, maybe it never would.

Chapter 17

The following day, Casey decided to face Chance
and tell him she knew about the ghosts that haunted
him. Honesty between them was the only way they
stood a chance at having any sort of relationship. Even
if that didn't work out, maybe talking about his past
would give him some peace of mind. The grief
counseling she'd gone through after Matt's death had
helped her get on with her life. She hadn't yet come to
terms with everything, but at least she'd picked up the
pieces. The pieces of Chance's grief still lay scattered.

He ate breakfast at the big house but kept his gaze
fixed on the plate of ham and eggs Billie set in front of
him. His expression remained closed.

Casey couldn't tell what he was thinking. The
tension reminded her of that first day in the café when
he'd sat hunched over his coffee, shutting out the rest of
the world. If she stayed here at the North Star, would he
someday shut her out?

Finished eating, Chance turned to his father. "I'm
going to the line shack today. Kyle said you want to
move a section of the herd up the mountain to graze the
rest of the summer. I've agreed to stay with them. Ed
will take over the irrigation dams, and Roy can work
with the mustangs." He waited for Justin's reply.

Casey stood at the counter, stirring cream into her
second cup of tea. She pretended not to hear. Trouble

was, she heard too well. And if the line shack was the cabin where they'd taken shelter during the storm earlier this summer, living in it didn't sound like a good idea.

"That place's got to be pretty rundown." Justin eyed his son, his silver-blue gaze running from Casey and back to Chance again. "I haven't been up there in a few years, but I'm sure it's in disrepair. We could haul a trailer up there."

"The cabin will be fine. I'll do a little repair while I'm there, patch the roof and chink the walls."

"You sure you want to do this?" Kyle pushed his own plate away. "I could send one of the other guys. It might be too much for you alone."

Was Kyle, for once, showing some concern for his brother?

"I'll be okay." Chance rose abruptly from the table. "I'll get my gear packed up and be ready to leave before noon. Maybe you could spare a man to help me drive those cows up there."

"I'll do that," Kyle said. "He'll meet you at the south pasture."

Chance nodded and stepped over the bench seat. He plucked his hat from the hook by the door and stopped by Billie where she stood wiping down the stove. "Would it be a problem to fix up a few supplies? I'll pack a mule with feed. I just need some groceries to tide me over 'til next week."

Billie's sharp glance flicked over the man. "I'll see to it." The older woman had long ago learned not to argue with the McCord men after they made up their minds.

Chance walked out the back door without even

saying goodbye.

Casey felt her heart sink like a stone in the river. Thank goodness Jamie had gone out to feed the pony and missed this conversation. When he learned Chance was gone and wouldn't return before they left for Michigan, he'd be devastated.

For two days, she kept busy cooking and serving meals and cleaning cabins. On the third day, Justin caught her in the study, where she was reading up for another campfire talk.

He took the book from Casey's hands and sat beside her on the leather sofa. "What I said about Chance still stands. He's a good man. He's just unsure of what he wants out of life anymore. He has his reasons."

"I know." Casey spared Justin the pain of relating the tragedy. "Billie told me about the accident. I understand what a terrible loss you all suffered and why Chance left that second time."

Justin stared down at his gnarled hands and waited a moment. "I'm sure you understand what a blow it dealt Chance. He finally couldn't cope with the loss anymore and took off for parts unknown. I'm still amazed he came back."

"He claims he's done running. Yet, he's gone off by himself again." Almost afraid to admit the truth, she swallowed hard. "I think maybe to avoid me."

Justin stroked his mustache. "I suppose in many ways he is still running. He just doesn't realize it, and none of us can help him."

Did Justin believe she could stop Chance from leaving again? "I'm not sure anything I say will matter now. He's afraid he can't be the kind of man I need.

I'm afraid, even if I stay, he might leave again one day. Until we both get past our fears, I don't hold out any hope for us."

Justin settled his silver-blue gaze on Casey. "Do you want to have that hope? Do you love him?"

For a long moment, Casey studied Justin's roughhewn face. Did she dare say the words out loud? Would speaking the words here make saying them to Chance easier? She looked away. "I love him very much."

"Then take your own advice. Go. Tell him. Don't let this shot at happiness pass you by, Casey. You're both young enough to start a new life together. Maybe you can even give that boy of yours a brother or sister or two."

She shook her head. "We haven't talked about how we really feel, let alone marriage, Justin."

He raised his shaggy eyebrows. "Then make him talk about it. You're a woman. Apply a few of those feminine wiles."

Casey lifted her hands, palms up. "Afraid I'm not very wily."

"But you're mighty pretty." Justin grinned and clasped one of her hands in his. "Forgive an old man's foolishness, but I'd like to see both of my sons settled and happy before it's my time to go. After that incident last spring, who knows where I'm headed next? Marianne is doing a good job of persuading Kyle to give up the single life. If you could convince Chance to settle down, maybe, between the two of you women, you'd get my sons together again."

Casey sighed. "Are you sure you're not just hankering for grandchildren?"

"There is that, too. Having Jamie around this summer has been a gift. Almost like…when Scottie was here. Riding that pony. Tagging after me." His mouth slanted in a crooked smile.

Casey leaned forward and gave Justin a quick kiss on the cheek.

He flushed and cleared his throat. "Forgive me for saying this, but you're a woman to make a man want to live again. That is something special. Don't throw away whatever chance you two might have together."

Had Justin ever thrown away such a chance with someone? His wife, Alicia, had died sixteen years ago, so maybe he was just an old man talking. "Do you think I can make Chance stay here for good?" Casey waited for his answer.

He jerked his head. "Darn right you can, but you won't do it sitting here running on with me. I'll have Roy or Ed take you to the cabin."

"No, that's okay. I think I can find it." No way did she want a wrangler taking her to the cabin in the hills.

"Billie and I can watch the boy, if you want to leave first thing in the morning. I'll have one of the boys saddle up Dakota." He put his hands on his knees. "I'm glad that's settled."

Casey bit her lip, then spoke her fear. "What if we're wrong, Justin?"

He grinned and winked the same way Chance did when in a teasing mood. "But what if we're right?"

That evening, Casey wandered to the corrals where, a few months ago, Chance had first kissed her in the falling twilight. Resting her arms on the top fence rail, she watched the sun set behind the mountains and remembered that moment and how her heart had raced.

Even then more than just a fleeting attraction existed between them, and now she faced a life-changing decision. Maybe riding to the cabin wouldn't give her an answer to the question that tugged at her heart, but she had to do it...or live with regrets.

****

Chance used a few choice words to coerce the camp stove into working. He'd hooked up a new propane tank, but the flame sputtered and flickered out. The first two nights up here, he'd heated coffee on the potbelly and eaten a cold dinner, too tired to bother lighting the stove. Now that he had a hankering for a hot meal, the damn thing wouldn't cooperate. One more unsuccessful attempt and he was sorely tempted to heave the metal beast out the door.

He held the match until it scorched his fingers, and then, with a few more colorful epithets, he gave up. If he kept at it, he might blow himself to kingdom come. But what did he expect? The stove had been sitting here a long time and was no doubt rusted from disuse. He threw down the box of matches and dug through the supplies Billie had sent—hard biscuits, canned corned beef hash, canned peaches, and jerky. What he wouldn't do now for one of Billie's and Casey's home-cooked meals. He'd gotten spoiled this summer and, for the moment, regretted his hasty decision to watch over the herd. Maybe he should've stayed and tried to work things out with Casey.

Casey. Just the thought of her sent a rush of fierce desire racing through him. Why had he let himself fall in love? Why hadn't he kept his distance? *Because falling for Casey was inevitable...and so easy.* From that first moment in the café, when a pretty woman wearing a college sweatshirt and skinny jeans with her mass of wavy hair pulled into a ponytail asked him to move over, he had the urge to let loose all that tawny hair and run his fingers through those waves. And once he did, Chance McCord was a goner. Not that other girls hadn't enticed him in the past five years, but this one…this one he couldn't get out of his head. And now, he ached to see her again and to hold her close and taste her kisses. Kissing Casey was like a taste of heaven. Except he'd probably blown that all to hell.

The cabin was anything but heaven—hot in the daytime, cold and miserable after the sun slid behind the mountains, and the bed a whole hell of a lot harder than he remembered. He'd been too numb then to notice. But after five years, the numbness had eased up, only to be replaced by a pain of a different sort. The pain of fitting into a mold he'd never wanted to wear.

As if coming home to the North Star didn't prove hard enough, he went and complicated his life further by falling in love. Then, like a fool, he'd treated Casey in a way no one should treat a woman. If she were smart, she'd forget all about him. Trouble was, he would never forget about her.

He eyed the potbelly stove. If he wanted to eat and stay halfway warm tonight, he better get some wood cut and stoke her up.

Outside, from her spot beneath the pine trees, Mariah watched him head for the woodpile. She'd insisted on coming along, as if she knew he needed someone looking out for him, as well as the cattle.

Grateful for her company, he called her, and she followed. Mariah was maybe the only being in the world who liked him the way he was and had no desire to change him. He set to chopping wood like his life depended on it, but even the hard physical work couldn't erase from his mind the image of Casey, as she stood at the kitchen counter, watching him walk out the door.

****

In the morning, Dakota waited patiently, saddled and bridled, at a hitching post near the barns. Scout, the flashy black-and-white Paint gelding Roy always rode, stood ready for riding, too.

"Why are you here, Scout?" Casey glanced about but didn't see any of the wranglers. *Good thing.* She wanted to clear out before anyone else saw her leave. Speaking in a hushed tone to the little mare, she lifted the saddlebags Billie had packed with food and placed them behind the saddle. Now she had to figure out how to attach them so they didn't fall off.

"Here, let me show you." Roy appeared beside her and lifted the leather strings hanging from the saddle. "You just pull these through the grommets on the bags and knot them up good and tight." He did one and stood back. "Now you try."

So much for leaving without someone noticing. Well, nothing to do about it now. She fumbled with the strings but finally got them tied on both sides of the saddle.

He gave her a thumbs-up. "Good job. You're a fast learner, Ms. Casey."

She smiled at the young wrangler's praise. "You're an excellent teacher, Roy. Thank you for saddling Dakota for me." With his black-as-obsidian eyes and long hair, he was a heck of a good-looking guy. She bet the girls in the valley thought so, too.

"You ready then?"

She unloosed the reins from the hitching post. "I am. I should make it to the cabin by noon." She pulled herself into the saddle.

Roy did the same on Scout.

"Are you heading out to work now?"

He didn't answer.

She gathered the reins and turned Dakota toward the trail leading behind the corrals and the cottonwood grove. She waited a moment, deciding which trail to take once they got into the hills, then clicked her tongue to urge the mare forward.

Roy rode up beside her and tipped his hat. "You can lead the way. I'll just follow along."

She drew back on the reins. "Wait, what do you mean? I'm fine. I don't need—"

"Yeah, well, Justin told me I need to go with you at least halfway, and truth is, they've spotted a few grizzlies in this area recently."

Grizzlies. The word sent a shiver zipping along Casey's spine, and the fear of facing up with a bear overrode her desire to keep this trip to the cabin secret. Anyway, no use arguing the matter. Word traveled on this ranch like wildfire. "Okay, we wouldn't want to upset Justin." She nudged the mare's sides, and Dakota headed out past the last corral.

Roy followed.

On the trail, clouds of dirt drifted around the horses' hooves and soon coated them all with a soft layer of dust. Despite the storms on the mountains, they'd had little rain in the valley this summer.

When the path widened some, Roy drew up alongside Casey. "Less dust in my face," he explained.

"I can't argue with that, but is it always so dry this late in the summer?"

Roy shrugged broad shoulders. "Not always, but the drought is getting worse. There was a fire the first year I worked at the North Star. Luckily, it didn't reach the ranch."

She peered at the surrounding forest, imagining the towering lodgepole pines on fire. "We see the reports about wildfires on TV at home. It must be terrifying for anyone in their path. I sure hope a fire never reaches the North Star."

"That would be a sad day," Roy agreed.

They rode on in silence, accompanied by the trills of songbirds and the brief cry of an eagle overhead. The pungent scent of the lodgepole pines permeated the summer day.

Casey mulled a question around in her head. "Do you think I'm foolish for doing this? Will it make any difference?" She glanced at Roy.

The wide brim of his hat hid his face well, but he shifted his hands over the reins. A few seconds passed. "Not for me to say, Ms. Casey. You do what you feel is right."

"But as another man, do you—?"

Roy halted Scout.

Casey did the same with Dakota. She met Roy's gaze. A glimmer of something burned in his dark eyes—a trace of some emotion she couldn't identify...or didn't want to.

Roy looked away toward the wild forest. "Guys like Chance, they have their own trail to ride. I haven't known him long, but I think you know him well enough to figure out what you want...and what your heart wants."

The wrangler had a way with words, and his words right now gave Casey much to think about as they rode on in silence.

The cabin came into sight, and he pulled Scout up again. "You can go on from here. You'll be all right. I hope this works out." Roy dropped back behind her on the trail.

Casey swiveled in her saddle. "Thanks for getting me here, Roy, and for being a friend when I've needed one."

For an answer, he touched the brim of his hat and nodded for her to go on.

Casey felt his gaze follow her before she heard him turn Scout around to head back down the trail.

In the clearing, Mariah bounded out to meet Casey and announce her arrival.

At a hitching post, Casey slid from the saddle and tipped her head to one side, listening for the sound of a man's voice. Chance wouldn't pasture the cattle this close to the cabin, but in a lush grassy area a little farther on. Perhaps that's where he was now with the herd, keeping them safe from bears…and whatever else lurked on the mountain. "Hey, girl." She held out a hand to the big dog. "Where's your cowboy?" The place seemed as deserted as it had that day of the storm.

Mariah sniffed her hand, then turned and disappeared around the side of the cabin.

Casey tethered Dakota to the post and followed the dog.

The sharp crack of an ax hitting wood echoed off the mountain and bounced back to the cabin. Afternoons were still summer-warm, but the mountain nights grew chilly, and he would need to keep the potbelly going to stay warm.

At the edge of the woods, Chance stood, legs braced wide apart. With his back turned, he raised his arms and swung the ax again.

Since she'd last seen him felt like forever, and Casey drank in the sight of his tall, sinewy frame. Memories of every kiss they'd shared drifted through her head. She bit her lips, remembering their taste. If only she'd known sooner about the past that haunted Chance. Things might not have proved so difficult between them.

With one fluid motion, he finished splitting the log and added it to the ones stacked neatly nearby. He stuck the ax in one log and paused to brush an arm across his forehead. The sun poured down on the mountain, and he'd pulled his plaid cotton shirt free from his jeans and rolled the sleeves past his elbows. His arms were brown from the sun.

With painful clarity, she could still feel the gentle touch of his embrace while the storm raged outside the cabin. Her heart tripped over itself, and she stopped to catch her breath. How could she confront Chance?

Figure out what your heart wants. That's what she had to do.

Chapter 18

Mariah gamboled up to Chance. He bent over to pet her, ruffling her furry neck. "What's up, old girl? What were you barking at? Did you hear something?"

The dog glanced past him.

Chance straightened swiftly and pivoted, scanning the clearing. He'd taken off his hat and perched it on a nearby stump. His dark hair lay rumpled up where he'd run a hand through it, and a two-day growth of beard shadowed his face.

The look on any other man would shout unkempt, but his darn sexy gaze cut across the clearing. Casey's heart pounded in her ears. All the way up the trail, she had rehearsed in her mind what to say, but now all the words deserted her. She could only stand and stare like some silly, moonstruck teenager.

He shuffled a little closer. "What are you doing here, Casey?"

Like softness over steel, his voice traveled across the clearing. Her knees threatened to buckle, but she hadn't ridden up a mountain to stand silent, and she sure as heck wasn't leaving without some answers. She cleared her throat. "I'm here because, as far as I'm concerned, it's not finished between us, and you avoiding me isn't the end."

Mariah ran back to Casey and whined.

She senses the tension. Casey touched Mariah's

furry head for courage. "I told you I'm afraid if Jamie and I should stay, you might leave again. I still am afraid, but I'll face that fear and deal with it…if you're willing to take on a woman who's shaking in her boots right now."

He dropped his chin to his chest and chuckled quietly. Then he plucked his hat from the stump and came to stand in front of her.

She raised her gaze. *Will he tell me to leave? Say our brief fling is over? Does he want me to go away?*

A wry smile lifted the corners of his mouth. "From that first day in Jackson, I knew you were one feisty lady. Beneath that sweet, feminine exterior lurked a bold woman."

Casey sniffed and lifted her chin. "And you could tell that how?"

"Not every woman would ask a stranger to move over…or come up a mountain to find a man. I'm flattered."

"Well, it's not flattery I intended, and I surely didn't come up here to joke about my feelings." Anger bubbled beneath her fear as she glared.

The smile left his face, and he moved toward her. "Does this look like I'm joking?"

She started to step back, but Chance caught her up with one arm and held her close. She lifted her face. He kissed her, and a flood of shock waves jolted through her senses. The scent of the pines and the wildflowers and the wood he'd been splitting filled her head, and once again only the two of them existed in the universe.

When he finally lifted his mouth from hers, he kissed each eyelid and murmured low and husky into her ear. "Tell me again you'll stay."

"I…will." Her own voice quivered. "I will stay, if you want us to."

"Because?"

Did she have to say it first? Looked that way. She stared at the pearl snaps on his wrinkled shirt, then at his face. "I think I love you?" His low groan vibrated against her. A sound of pleasure or despair?

"Is that a for sure?"

She nodded. "Yeah, it's a for sure." Would he say it now? Or did he still doubt his feelings?

He touched her hair. "Why? Why are you sure?"

She blew out a breath. What an exasperating man. But he deserved an honest answer. "You befriended a little boy and made his dream of riding a pony come true. I know you had a reason for leaving. You ran from a heartbreaking tragedy." Beneath her hands, the muscles in his chest tightened.

He leaned away. A frown flickered across his face. "So, you know?"

She sighed. "Billie told me about Angela and Scottie. I'm so sorry, Chance. I had no idea what you'd been through. I understand now why you had to leave." She watched his eyes darken to the color of the rushing Snake River.

"I don't need pity, Casey, nor even understanding anymore. What I need is to move on and find a reason to live again." He swallowed hard and looked away.

She disentangled herself from his arms and sat on a tree stump. "I know what you mean. I had to do that, too, after Matt died. I remember hurting so badly, I just wanted to curl up and die. Some days, it was all I could do to get out of bed and make breakfast. If not for Jamie, I probably wouldn't have gotten up at all."

Chance's face took on a distant look. His hands clenched, and a nerve twitched in his cheek.

No doubt, those scattered pieces of grief were floating around him right now. Would he dare to pick them up?

He swiped a hand across his face. "At least, you had your son and a reason to go on. I had nothing, Casey. *Nothing.*"

His pain-wracked words cut through Casey like a razor's edge. She struggled to hold back tears, feeling the grief she had known but also now some of his. She took a deep breath and steadied her voice. "Maybe you felt you had nothing, but now you have me…and Jamie. He loves you, too."

His gaze rested on her. "What about your job in Michigan? And your family there?"

Deep sorrow still resided in his heart, and she wanted so much to make his life—and hers—better. "If I'm ever to recover from my loss, I need a new life. I want to start here."

"Then you'd stay on at the North Star?"

"If you would. If you promise never to leave again."

He took her hand and pulled her from the stump. "Between the wild horses and a woman who's gotten under my skin, I better stay put. I won't leave the North Star, if you don't." He put his arms around her and lifted her until her boots brushed the tops of his. "That is a promise I intend to keep." He bent his head and kissed her.

For a while, the only thought in Casey's head was how perfectly they fit together.

Mariah woofed a warning followed by alarmed

whickers from Dakota and Smoky.

Chance let Casey slide down his body until her feet touched the ground. "Something's up with the horses." He turned toward the small pen off the lean-to where Mariah stood at silent attention. He stooped to pick up both their hats where they had fallen and shoved Casey's hat into her hands. "You best get into the cabin while I check to see what's going on."

She hesitated. "What is it you think?"

"Just go." He gave her a gentle push.

Casey hung back while Roy's words played over in her head. *They've spotted grizzlies up here.* A zip of fear prickled her backbone. "Chance, you shouldn't—"

"Casey, honey, when we're out here and I ask you to move, please do it and don't ask questions." He motioned toward the cabin. "Now go."

"But there's food in the saddlebags and—"

His frown allowed no argument.

She headed for the cabin. Once inside, she flashed back to the day they'd taken shelter here. Not much had changed, except for the sleeping bag spread out on the single bunk and a few cans of food stacked beside the ancient camp stove. The day's heat penetrated the log walls, so she shed her jacket and hung it and her hat on a hook by the door. How could anyone live in this place? The idea was beyond her wildest imagination.

She wandered from one window to the other and peered out, but dust and grime still covered the glass. She listened for any sounds of distress. Nothing. What was going on out there? What if a bear lurked around the cabin? What if it…?

Desperate to tamp down her fear, Casey crossed to the table and brushed some crumbs into her hand. She looked around for a trash can. None, but she saw a small sink with a pump handle. She dumped the crumbs there and contemplated pumping water into the sink that held a dirty cup, plate, and eating utensils. Maybe she could wash them. She gripped the handle to give it a crank, but Mariah's deep bark just outside the cabin made her jump. Behind her, the door swung open. Was a bear charging inside? She grabbed a knife from the sink and whirled, prepared to face the threat.

Chance slammed the door and held up an arm in front of him. "Whoa, remind me to never make you mad."

Casey dropped the knife into the sink and sagged against the counter. "You scared the heck out of me." She held a hand over her heart. "Did you see anything?"

He slid the bolt on the door and set the saddlebags on the table. "I didn't, but I put Dakota in the lean-to with Smoky and the mule."

"What about Mariah?" She was a big dog, but against a predator, Mariah might not stand a chance.

"She's right by the door, doing her duty as a guardian. That's what she's bred to do. Once she knows we're okay, she'll head on down to the cattle." He studied Casey's face a moment, then took off his hat and pulled out a chair by the table. "You better sit down. You're a little pale."

She sat and didn't argue.

He pumped water into the sink and filled a cup. "Here, drink this." He handed it over.

She eyed the cup.

"Don't worry. It's clean." He winked and turned to check out the saddlebags, setting the canned goods and a package of fresh biscuits on the table. "This is definitely better than what I'd planned for dinner."

"What did you plan?" He hadn't taken much when he left.

"Probably would've gone fishing in Antler Creek. We always took out some nice-sized trout." He slid one biscuit from the package and, splitting it in two, popped half in his mouth. "Light as a feather. Billie sure knows how to make them."

Casey watched a look of pure satisfaction cross his face as he chewed and swallowed. She bristled and stood to put away the groceries in the small cupboard. "That might be true, but I'll have you know I made those just this morning."

He sidled up behind her and put his arms around her middle. "Cookies. Biscuits. I guess they're another good reason to keep you at the North Star. Just in case Billie ever decides to retire."

"I'm not sure that will ever happen. She's—"

He moved her hair aside and pressed a kiss on the side of her neck.

Casey's pulse went into overdrive, and she leaned against him.

He turned her and lifted her chin. "I'm sorry if I sounded harsh out there. I didn't mean to scare you. But you need to be aware this country is different from what you're used to. Just because I didn't see something doesn't mean it wasn't there."

She tipped her head. "Like a bear?"

A small smile lifted his mouth. "Yep, like a bear, and speaking of staying safe, how did you manage to sneak away from the ranch without Justin or Billie finding out? I can't imagine they would've let you come up here alone."

"They didn't. Roy rode with me until I could see the cabin." She noticed a flicker of some strange emotion darkened Chance's eyes for a second but was quickly squelched and replaced by a teasing light.

"I think that young wrangler has a thing for you, Ms. Casey."

The comment followed by how Roy always addressed her gave Casey a start. "Whatever are you talking about?"

He let her go and finished the biscuit. "Roy Silver Wolf has taken a shine to you. He's smitten."

Casey didn't quite know what to say. She and Roy had become pretty good friends over the summer, but she'd never given him any reason to think their friendship was anything more. Besides, he knew how she felt about Chance. "That's crazy. Why would you even say such a thing?"

He shrugged. "I reckon because it's true. The attraction probably started before I even arrived. Teaching you to drive the truck and ride a horse and now coming up here today."

Casey waved away his comments. "But Justin told him to do all that, and how did you even know about the truck and the riding?" She saw his wry amusement.

"Haven't you learned anything at the North Star this summer? Nothing is secret. At least, not for long. Everybody knows everybody's business, for better or for worse. And once the ranch knows, the whole darn valley knows."

The truth of Chance's statement gave her a taste of bittersweet reality. If she stayed to make a new life, could she cope with all that her decision entailed—the inherent dangers, the isolation, the hardships? The way they all had to depend on one another. Knowing whether you could trust someone might make the difference between life and death here. She had learned to trust Roy's honest and open nature, but she'd never wanted him to feel anything but friendship for her. "But he's so young, and…and I never meant—"

"Of course you didn't. Casey, honey, it's okay. You're right. He's young. Tomorrow, some girl at the rodeo will catch his eye. But here's something you can believe is true. None will catch mine. I'm smitten, too." He picked up his hat and jammed it on his head. "And now Smoky, Mariah, and I are going out to check on those cows. You can stay here where it's nice and safe."

Casey followed him and plucked her own hat from the hook by the door. "I'd rather come with you. If I stay in Wyoming, I guess I better get the hang of ranch life besides cooking and cleaning cabins."

They spent the next several hours circling the herd that grazed in the mountain pasture. She listened to the soft lowing of the cows and the trill of the songbirds, the jingling of the horses' bridles, and the occasional shriek of a predator bird from high above. Could she get used to this life? Would leaving behind the only kind of life she'd ever known give her the new start she needed? Was her decision too hasty? A lot of questions, but she only had to watch the man riding beside her to have her answer. If living here meant she would see Chance every day for the rest of her life, that was answer enough.

The sun hovered over the mountain peaks when they returned to the cabin. Golden rays stretched out across the wide Wyoming sky before disappearing behind the Tetons.

Casey slid from her saddle, her legs wobbling from the long day of riding. She would have led Dakota into the lean-to but turned and saw Chance beside her.

He took the reins. "You go ahead inside. I'll get the horses fed and settled for the night. Maybe if I start a fire in the wood stove, you can cook us up dinner from those supplies you brought along. I don't know about you, but I'm starving."

Casey washed in the small sink and opened the cans of corned beef hash. She couldn't light the camp stove the first few times and finally set about cleaning the burners that hadn't seen use in a long while. A dozen spent matches later, she lit the burners. In a short time, she had hash sizzling in the fry pan and a pot of coffee perking.

Chance hustled through the doorway with an armload of chopped wood. "I'll get a fire started and…hey, what's cooking? How did you—"

"The stove just needed a good cleaning is all." Casey tossed him a smug smile. "Now, put your wood over there and wash your hands."

"Yes, ma'am. I mean, yes, Ms. Casey."

She stuck out her tongue and stirred the hash.

"Getting a little sassy, aren't we?" He washed at the sink and dried his hands on a frayed towel. "Where did my favorite librarian learn to clean a camp stove?"

She motioned for him to sit at the table and set two plates full of food there, placing the biscuits beside them. "Matt and I camped a lot when we first married. We didn't have much money to vacation anyplace fancy. He showed me how to take care of our equipment." The memory of a trip they'd taken to the

Upper Peninsula of Michigan popped into her mind. Matt loved the waterfalls they'd seen and the big lakes. He talked even then about moving to the U.P. someday. If only he hadn't flown his plane up there and met with a late autumn storm on the way home.

Chance hesitated before digging into his dinner. "Casey, honey, what's wrong?"

She shook the memory away and forced a smile. "Oh, nothing. Let's eat before everything gets cold. I have some dessert for us." After dinner, Casey opened the second saddle bag pouch. "The brownies aren't too mashed. I think they're still edible."

His eyes lit up. "Oh heck, I'll eat them even if they're mashed. Got anymore coffee? It'll keep me up all night, but that's okay. I need to listen in case the cows start bellowing."

Casey finished her brownie, relishing the last chocolaty bite. Outside the cabin, daylight sank into deep purple until the darkness prevented her from riding back down the mountain. She checked the signal bars on her phone and saw none. "I should've left sooner. Jamie's probably worried, and what will Billie think?"

"She'll think you're here with me, and that I wouldn't let you leave by yourself." Chance picked up their dishes and carried them to the sink. "How about I clean up and you can take a shower, if you like."

Casey brightened. "A shower? Here?"

"Sure. It's not totally deer camp, where nobody washes. There are towels by the bunk over there. Help yourself. The shower's nothing glamorous, but it feels pretty good after a day in the saddle."

Outside the cabin, the shower boasted a respectful

wall, but the pull chain to release the water gave her pause. Yep, this was deer camp, but she had little choice unless she went to sleep gritty. She wasted no time stripping out of her jeans, shirt, and underwear. Shivering in the cool night air, she yanked the chain. The water proved a tad cold, even after a day of the tank sitting in the sun. Casey didn't dawdle. She found a bar of soap and washed herself to her toes. After rinsing, she dried herself off and wrapped the faded terrycloth around her body.

Chance appeared with a flannel shirt. He hung it outside the shower enclosure and turned away. "It's wrinkled but clean."

The tails of the shirt ended just above her knees. Casey slipped on her underwear and buttoned up the shirt as she made her way through a back door and into the cabin, now lit by a glowing lantern and warmed by a fire in the wood stove. She hung the towel to dry and ran her fingers through her tangled hair. "I don't suppose you have a brush here somewhere."

Chance produced a wide-tooth comb.

Casey took it with a smile. "This reminds me of the one my mom used when I was a kid. When she combed my hair, we always had a battle. We fought a lot even then."

After watching her make several attempts to tug at the snarls, Chance sat her down and gently slid the comb through her hair until the strands lay tangle-free upon her shoulders.

"Where did you learn to do that?" she asked, and then wished she could take it back. Did she really want to know?

He set the comb aside and went to the door,

opening it to go outside. A gust of wind blew past him.

Casey grabbed her jacket and followed. Even in the solid darkness of the mountain night, she read a trace of sadness in the slant of his mouth and the set of his jaw. A glimmer shone in his eyes. She touched his arm. "I'm sorry. I shouldn't have asked. You don't have to answer."

He shoved his hands into his pockets. "Angela liked me to do that for her when she was expecting Scottie. She didn't always feel well and sometimes...sometimes, she barely got out of bed."

Casey recognized his pain and that the words were hard for him to say. She slipped her hand into the crook of his elbow and leaned her head on his arm. "Was it a difficult pregnancy?"

He shrugged against her. "Yeah, I guess. I was young then. Hell, what did I know? But even afterwards, after Scottie was born, Angie had...issues."

Postpartum depression? Casey didn't press for more but lifted her gaze to the sky now filled with a myriad of twinkling stars. At the tip of the Little Dipper's handle, the North Star winked above them. Had the early McCord settlers named their ranch after it? "Somewhere is a star called Casey. Matt had one named after me. He said a star was the best wedding gift he could give me. He dreamed of flying among the stars."

Chance shifted and slipped an arm around her shoulders. "How did he die, Casey? You've never said."

A sad pain rippled through her. She'd never talked about it to anyone other than her family and the grief counselor. "Matt was a pilot. He flew small planes, taking people where they needed to go. In November, almost three years ago, he flew some hunters to Michigan's Upper Peninsula. On the way back, he ran into a storm, a fierce squall. His plane went down." She couldn't finish. The truth was too hard to think about. The reality was still too cruel.

Chance drew her closer. "I'm sorry you went through that. I guess we've both had some tough times."

"He wanted to be an astronaut. That was his dream since he was a kid, but we got married right out of college. He became a pilot, but I always wondered…"

"If you held him back?"

How did he know? That she was convinced if she and Matt hadn't met, he would have gone on to greater things…and maybe still be alive. Casey sighed. "The worst thing is, we argued that day. I didn't want him to go. We had bad weather predicted, but Matt loved adventure. He promised me he'd be all right, but before he left, I said some awful things. I said he loved flying more than he loved Jamie and me."

"I'm sure it wasn't true."

"At that moment, I believed it was. Those words have haunted me ever since."

The wind picked up and blew over the mountain, accompanied by a dip in temperature and the scent of rain. Beneath her jacket and the shirt, Casey shivered. Was it from the night air or the truth she'd spoken?

"You best go inside," Chance murmured. "You can take the bunk."

"What will you do?"

"Hang out here for a while. In the morning, I'll ride back with you. Ed is supposed to meet me with more supplies. I might have to stay with the herd another few weeks."

No sense in arguing. Once the man made his mind up to something, he would do it. If she stayed in Wyoming, she needed to get used to that and to a different way of life. Did she know what she was getting into? Maybe her answer, along with the rain, would come before morning.

Chapter 19

Casey jolted awake with a ragged ache in her back. An unfamiliar sound drifted from outside—a thin howl floating in the night, followed by a mournful chorus. She turned on the hard bunk and listened. Silence. Then wind buffeted the cabin walls. A moment later, the much-needed rain drummed against the windows. A flash of sulfur-yellow lightning illuminated the room, followed by a deep rumble of thunder. She bolted up. Orienting herself to the shadowy surroundings, she tossed the sleeping bag away and swung her legs to the side of the bunk. Where had Chance gone off to? She'd heard him come inside and go into the shower before she fell asleep. Was he checking on the cattle? Without regard for his own safety, had he headed into a storm...just like Matt? A lump of sick fear lodged in her throat.

This time, when the door opened, she didn't have a knife in her hand, but a flood of relief poured through her veins. She yanked the shirt to cover her knees and met Chance's gaze.

He plucked off his hat and shook the rain from the brim. "I'm sorry. Did I wake you? I tried to be quiet." He shrugged out of his denim jacket and hung it and his hat on the hook. "Just wanted to check on the horses and make sure the lean-to was closed up."

He would worry about the horses. Maybe the work,

the ranch, would always come first in their lives. Could she handle that? "The storm woke me." She rubbed at the twinge in her back. "Although that bunk is hard as cement."

He grinned and pulled off his boots on the bootjack. "It does leave a lot to be desired. Sorry I can't offer any better accommodations."

"It's okay. I asked for it." Casey rubbed her flannel-sleeved arms and wandered to stand next to the wood stove that still emanated heat. On her first trip to the cabin, she was afraid the stove would explode. Another snap of lightning and a crack of thunder made her jump. "Sounds like the storm is right over us. Is it always that way up here?"

"Usually." He lifted the coffeepot he'd left on the wood stove and shook it. "Want some? Guaranteed to keep you awake the rest of the night." He emptied the potent brew into the two mugs and handed one to Casey, touching the rim of his mug to hers. "Here's to strong coffee and warm cabins that give us shelter in the storm."

She wrapped her hands around the mug. "Is that a little cowboy poetry?"

He winked. "Yep. I made it up just for you."

Casey sipped the bitter coffee and made a face. "My dad and Matt always said my coffee had a kick. I guess they were right."

Chance drained his mug and set it aside. "I kinda like it myself. It's got that special Casey touch. I can get used to it."

She dumped the rest in the sink and turned around...and met Chance's midnight gaze. The darkness surrounded them, and the storm rumbled overhead. The cabin suddenly grew smaller. Casey's pulse thrummed like the beating of a butterfly's wings. She bit her lip and took a breath for courage. "A while ago you said something…something about why you'd stayed away from me. Do you remember? It was because—"

"I wanted to make love to you?" He stepped closer and gently touched Casey's cheek, running the back of his fingers across her skin.

She pressed her palms against his shirtfront. "Do you still want to do that?" She waited for his answer while the awareness she'd known the moment they met in the café hummed between them.

"More than you know."

Her skin quivered at the sound of his hushed voice. But was his wanting her enough? Would it keep them together through the tough times? Through the worst of winter?

"But it's more than that, Casey. What I feel is something I can't say I've ever felt before, and I will do whatever it takes to hold on to it."

Did this mean what she hoped? "And you'd never leave?"

He took her face in his hands. "I told you, if you were my wife, I would never do that. Marriage is one commitment I believe in honoring."

The word *marriage* rolled around in Casey's head. "But you never said anything about my being your wife."

"Well, I'm saying it now." He kissed her, slipping his callused fingers through her hair. "I'm saying it now. Stay here and marry me, Casey. I'll care for you and the boy. You need never worry that I'll leave. I'd rather die first."

"Hush!" She leaned back and touched her fingertips to his lips. "Please promise me you won't do that, either. Not for a long, long time."

He laughed, then drew her closer and lifted her off her feet. "I promise," he whispered against her lips.

The urgency of the kiss that followed left Casey limp, and she clung to his arms.

They drifted to the bunk, but Casey would have none of lying there and pulled the sleeping bag onto the floor. "It can't be any harder than that rock." She spread the sleeping bag out, the extra blanket, and then added the single pillow. "I guess we'll have to share." She sank down onto the floor and drew him to sit. "Is this okay?"

He hesitated. "I didn't come prepared, you know. I mean…" He blew out a breath. "Two months in the hospital and rehab, I got tested for everything under the sun, and then I spent a few more months at Hank's home. What I'm saying, Casey-honey, is there hasn't been anyone since then, but I didn't expect—"

"It's okay." Casey curled one hand inside of his. "There's been no one for me since Matt. I—"

"Hush." He eased her back on the sleeping bag and kissed her chin and the side of her neck and slipped the top buttons of the shirt free but stopped until she opened her eyes. "Whatever happens here tonight, Casey, happens. I only need to know one thing. Am I a stand-in? When you look at me, who do you see?"

Her gaze locked with his. "I guess that depends. Who do you see? A ghost from the past?"

She shivered as he trailed his fingers down her throat, stopping at her collarbone and stroking the vulnerable spot with his thumb.

"No ghosts. Only a woman I want to spend the rest of my life getting to know."

A small smile touched her mouth before she hooked her hands around his neck. "Then I see a man who'll always be my favorite cowboy. That's a promise."

When did he say the words she ached to hear? Maybe as the storm abated and the lightning flickered away. Or when the wind drifted in soft sighs through the pine trees. For sure, when he whispered against her skin, and every touch like sweet fire swept deep down into her soul.

"I love you, Casey. I always will. Never doubt that."

Later, in the stillness of the early morning, contentment filled her heart. She couldn't resist leaning over to press a kiss to his whiskery cheek while he slept. How had they found each other? Two people who were so different and from two opposite walks of life. They'd both been through so much. Did they stand a chance at staying together? Life with Chance would not be without its trials. *But I can do this. If he's here, that's all I need.*

****

Chance led Dakota from the lean-to and handed Casey the reins. "All saddled up and ready for you. How're you doing this morning…okay?"

Their conversation after rising had been stilted. Neither of them was quite sure of what to say after the night of passion they shared. Casey glanced up and then averted her gaze. "I'm fine. No worries. I guess we should get on the trail. Ed is meeting you?"

"Yeah, halfway, then he'll ride with you the rest of the way."

She slid her hand along the mare's warm neck and rested it on the saddle horn.

"Need help?"

"No, sir. If you didn't notice yesterday, I can do this myself now." She started to pull herself into the saddle.

Chance stopped her, resting his hands lightly on her shoulders. "Casey, honey, what I said last night I meant, every single word. With my whole heart. Do you believe me?"

She did, but the light of day allowed common sense to raise its practical head, and she held back an answer.

"Are you having second thoughts about staying?"

His question, so softly spoken, echoed in her head. Was she? Did making such a huge change in her life not sound like a good idea? But his words from the night before crept into her muddled thoughts. *Marry me, Casey.* Had she dreamed that? "Did you...did you ask me to marry you? Last night. Did you..."

He slid his hands down her arms and kept her between him and Dakota. "I did ask you. But if I remember rightly, you never answered."

What more could she ask? He'd promised to stay, and love her, and marry her, and take care of Jamie. Coming from a man who'd run away from life and the people who loved him the most, his words surprised her. Could she trust that he'd changed? For her?

"Casey?"

He'd asked her to believe in him once before, on the day he offered to teach Jamie to ride. Now, he was asking for so much more, and, in her heart, Casey knew what she had to do. "Yes," she said. "My answer is yes." She dropped the reins and turned, standing on tiptoe and brushing her lips over his, then leaning in with more purpose.

Chance pressed her against Dakota's side and deepened the kiss, coaxing Casey to respond.

She returned the kiss with a passion she never believed was possible. Caught between Dakota's warm body and Chance's, Casey about melted from the heat of the kiss. She grasped his arms and held on tight.

Mariah woofed a warning.

Casey broke off the kiss and peered around Chance.

Ed strode toward them, leading his horse. He halted. A flush darkened his face.

She pushed Chance away. "Ed's here."

Chance frowned and glanced over his shoulder. "Little early, aren't you, Ed?" He didn't turn but grabbed Dakota's reins and tucked them into her hand.

Ed snatched off his hat and slapped it against his thigh. He looked away, then back again. "Sorry, Chance. Hate to interfere, but your brother sent me. It's your dad. They've taken Justin to the hospital in town."

"What? What are you talking about?" Chance shot Casey a glance.

Confused, she shook her head. Justin was fine when they last spoke. Or was he? *What did I miss?* She should have paid more attention, instead of worrying about her own problems.

"I left as Kyle and Billie were getting him in the truck. They're going to meet the ambulance halfway. I came to get you as fast as I could." Ed fingered the brim of his hat. "I have to tell you. The old man didn't look good. You ought to get right on home. I'll stay here for now."

Casey noted Ed's distressed frown. The young wrangler hated giving them this news. All the ranch hands had a special respect for Justin.

Chance still didn't move.

She grabbed his arm and yanked. "Come on, we need to go. Get Smoky."

Her touch brought him around, and in a few minutes, they headed down the trail to the North Star. The entire ride, her mind spun with scenarios of what they'd find when they reached the ranch.

Chapter 20

Casey entered the ranch house through the back door. Where was Jamie? He must be so afraid. A strange silence filled the empty rooms. No Billie cooking up a storm in the kitchen, although a bowl of half-peeled potatoes and carrots sat on the counter. No Justin prowling the rooms or working on his book in the study. Had he been at his desk when he suffered the attack?

She was about to call out her son's name, but voices drifted from the front porch. Opening the heavy oak door, she found Roy and Jamie sitting together on the swing. The young cowboy patted the tearful little boy's shoulder.

Jamie scooted off the swing and fled into her arms.

She knelt and held him. A rush of guilt swept through her for leaving Jamie to deal with this situation. *I should have been here.*

"Oh, Mom, an awful thing happened!" He sobbed against her shoulder. "M-Mr. McCord was goin' with me to watch Roy work with the mustangs. Then, he just groaned and fell. Said he couldn't breathe and for me to get Kyle. I did, Mom. Right away! But they hadda take him to the hosp-hospital." Jamie hiccupped loudly.

"I know, sweetie. Hush now. It's all right." Casey hugged the boy and stroked his hair much like the day when she told him his father was never coming home.

"You did the right thing and were very brave not to panic."

"But will Mr. McCord be all right?" Jamie lifted his tear-stained face from Casey's shirtfront. "I'm scared he's gonna die...like Dad did."

"I know." Casey wiped the tears from his cheeks. "We're all a little scared right now, but we just have to wait and see what happens." She glanced at Roy. "Is it his heart?"

His black eyes reflected a deep sadness. "Most likely, but he could walk to the truck, at least." He kept his gaze focused on Casey for a moment, then quickly looked away.

Remembering what Chance said about the wrangler having a thing for her, she searched for the right words. "Well, thank goodness for that. And thank you, for watching Jamie. I hope he wasn't any trouble."

"Nah, he's okay. I have a half-brother about his age." He snatched his hat from the porch railing. "Just hope the boss man's all right."

"I hope he gets to come home, and we can stay here so I can take care of him." Jamie stared at Casey. "Can we stay?"

"Don't worry about that." Casey gave the boy another hug. She didn't dare tell him about Chance asking her to marry him...nor about her answer.

Chance walked up the porch steps, and his stormy blue gaze met hers. Anxiety and pain brimmed in his eyes. He had stopped at the bunkhouse and changed into clean jeans and a dark blue shirt. He held his hat in his hands and stared down at Casey.

She felt him reach out for her support and rising, she grasped his hand. "It's going to be all right." She tried to convince him, as she had Jamie. "Why don't you let Roy drive you into town? I'd go, but somebody needs to stay and feed everyone."

Roy left the swing and tugged on his hat. "I can do that, Chance."

Chance waved away the wrangler's offer. "The place is short-handed enough with Kyle and me gone and Ed up to summer pasture now. You tend to the guests and help Casey with anything she needs."

For the first time since arriving at the North Star, he showed some authority as a McCord son.

"Will do." Roy flicked his dark gaze between them. "You can take Juanita." He tossed Chance the keys to his vehicle and left the porch.

Chance turned to Casey. "I'll call you as soon as I know anything." He grasped her hands and gave them a quick squeeze. "You stick with your mom," he spoke to Jamie. "She's going to need a lot of help today."

"I will, Chance." Jamie hugged him around one leg.

Chance rested a big hand on the boy's head for a moment, and then he leaned down and kissed Casey swiftly on the lips. "I wish you were coming with me," he whispered. "But I appreciate your holding things together here."

"And I will. But please let me know how Justin is doing. Your father…means a lot to me." She choked over the last words, hating the thought the old cowboy might never know he'd gotten his wish for her to stay at the North Star.

Chance nodded, kissed her again, and was gone.

Jamie clung to Casey. "He kissed you, Mom. Does that mean we can stay here?"

Casey met Jamie's somber gaze. "We'll talk about it later. Right now, we need to put together some lunch for the wranglers and the guests who might stop by. Can you help me?"

"Sure. Let's make peanut butter sandwiches. I heard Roy tell Ed he really likes peanut butter. Then I'll go out and help fill the water troughs. I want to make Chance proud of me." He took Casey's hand and led her to the kitchen.

She breathed a bittersweet sigh. In a matter of minutes, Jamie had turned from tearful to determined. Her little boy was growing up.

By the time they put away the supper dishes, they'd still had no phone call from the hospital. Casey remained at the big house. She read to Jamie for a while and allowed him to curl up beside her on the sofa.

Outside, the wind picked up and moaned through the pine trees.

She dozed for perhaps an hour and awoke when car doors slammed and raised voices echoed outside. In the next minute, Chance, Kyle, and Marianne entered through the front door. Their faces were haggard from lack of sleep and worry, but were not, thank goodness, torn with grief.

"I'm sorry I didn't call." Chance took Casey in his arms and gave her a fierce hug. "We just didn't know what was going to happen, and I couldn't call from Intensive Care. I should have had Marianne call, but I wasn't thinking clearly."

"It's okay." Casey patted his arm and felt the day's tension that still lurked in his tight muscles. "But how is Justin?" She glanced past him. "Where's Aunt Billie?"

"Justin is stable. He'll need surgery, but he's

holding his own. Billie is still at the hospital. They only allow one person, and she refused to leave."

Billie's staying didn't surprise Casey. She'd known for some time Billie cared about Justin. "You must all be exhausted and hungry. I'll make some coffee and sandwiches if one of you men will carry my son to bed."

"I'll put him in my room," Kyle offered. "I doubt I'll get much sleep tonight."

Marianne followed Casey down the hallway to the kitchen.

Casey pulled her aside. "Maybe you should stay with the guys. Make sure they're okay." A crackling tension between Chance and Kyle had hung in the air the minute they entered the house. If left alone, they might come to blows. Perhaps Marianne's presence would have a calming effect.

She was arranging the roast beef sandwiches and a full pot of coffee on a tray when that electric tension erupted.

Marianne met Casey in the hallway, her hazel eyes filled with tears. "Oh, Casey, hurry! They're at each other and saying awful things. I tried to make Kyle stop, but he's convinced this is all Chance's fault."

Balancing the tray, Casey sped along the hallway.

In the living room, Kyle gripped the back of a chair.

Chance stood at the fireplace with one arm braced on the mantel.

By the rigid set of his shoulders, she knew Chance held himself back from letting Kyle have it. Setting the tray on the coffee table, she turned and pointed toward the sandwiches. "Why don't you all have something to eat? I think you'll feel—"

"Well, brother, I hope you're satisfied now you got Dad laid up again," Kyle broke in. "He was doing fine 'til you came back, but that put him under a pretty bad strain. Course, you probably don't believe any of that. You never did think of anybody but yourself and what you wanted. Now, just because you want to come home, you do it, no matter what grief it causes anybody else."

"I don't see what grief it's caused you." Chance kept his voice low and even. "You're still in charge around here. I haven't challenged that."

"That's just it," Kyle spat out. "You never did see. You never realized what your selfishness did to us."

Chance wheeled about and faced Kyle. "Don't push me, little brother. If it's a fight you want, then I'm in the right mood tonight."

"Then let's not wait any longer." Kyle stepped away from the chair. He lifted his fists and advanced on Chance. His face contorted with cold hard anger.

Casey's heart pounded. More than worry about their father tore the brothers apart. Their conflict went back five years; a conflict they'd never settled. For it to come to a head now, while Justin lay in the hospital so ill, would solve nothing, but would only add more pain and division to a family already fractured. Before either man could raise a fist, she stepped between them, clutching Chance's arm. "You're not doing this. Not in your father's house. The two of you ought to be ashamed. Instead of being thankful your father is still alive, you're ready to tear each other apart. Isn't there any way you can talk about this peaceably?"

"No way I know of," Chance growled. "What's

between my brother and me is something I can never forgive."

What Chance still believed about Kyle wasn't pretty. Casey hated to force the truth out in the open, but somebody had to do it if the two were ever to reconcile. "What did he do that is so unforgiveable?" The bold question fell from Casey's mouth, and she waited for the repercussion.

Chance clenched his jaw and glared at Kyle. "He fell in love with my wife," he ground out.

Casey heard the pain in his voice from living with the years of grief.

"*What?*" Marianne's voice rose an octave. "How can that be true?" Her gaze darted between the brothers.

Chance turned back to the fireplace, bracing one booted foot against the cold hearth stones.

Casey watched a shudder run through him. More than anything, she wanted to offer him comfort. But Chance needed to conquer this on his own. The two men must resolve their conflict once and for all. She turned and hurried to the kitchen.

A few seconds later, Chance followed. He stood beside her and raked a hand through his hair. "I'm sorry you have to get dragged into my dysfunctional family's mess."

Casey's heart broke for what he'd been through, but she knew what she had to say. "Every family has its issues, and I'm sorry yours has suffered so much. But if it's always going to be this way, I can't stay here." She dared to face him, her eyes tearing. "When you and Kyle get things straight, then maybe I'll think about making the North Star our home. I love you, Chance, but I won't stay and raise Jamie in the middle of so much conflict. I can't stay while the shadow of Angela hangs over all of you."

Chance walked a few feet away, then pivoted back. "But we wouldn't have to stay here. We could go someplace else and raise Jamie. I can find work on another ranch. I'm not a total wipeout."

His anguish tore through Casey. She touched his whiskery cheek and sighed. "That's no answer, Chance, and you know it. You'd never be truly happy."

He grabbed her hand, lacing his fingers with hers. "Don't go, Casey. I need you."

Coming from such a prideful man, the admittance was almost more than Casey could bear. Tears slipped down her face one by one. "Then put Angela to rest. Make peace between you and Kyle. Forgive all the pain you've caused each other."

He ran one hand over his raspy chin and took a deep breath, exhaling slowly. "Come back in there with me. Please?"

Still holding his hand, Casey returned to the living room. Once there, she let go and perched on the arm of one chair.

Chance joined Kyle, where he stood alone in the middle of the room. "Sit down, Kyle. I guess it's time we talked." Chance motioned toward the sofa. "We're going to say what we should have said five years ago. We might not like each other any better when we're done, but at least, we'll know the truth. Then Angie can rest in peace. She doesn't deserve to be remembered this way, with so much pain and anger."

"Maybe I should leave." Marianne darted a tentative glance between the brothers. "If you'd rather this was private."

Plainly, Marianne didn't want to hear what the brothers said.

Out of fear of having Kyle's image tarnished?

Kyle shook his head and drew Marianne to the sofa. "I'd rather you stayed." Propping his elbows on his knees, Kyle clasped his hands between them and stared at the floor.

Chance took the easy chair with Casey sitting on the arm. He grasped her hand again. "I'm going to ask what I should have asked after Angela died. What happened that day, Kyle? Why did you go with Angie?"

Kyle rubbed one fist against the other hand and studied his brother before answering. "Not for the reason you've always thought. It's true I loved Angie. She was just too easy to love. Although I guess for you that wasn't true."

Chance leaned forward and scowled. "What do you mean?"

Anger flared in Kyle's eyes again. "I mean, you obviously didn't care about her at all. I hated you for that. I still do for ignoring her after Scottie was born. Maybe you resented giving up the rodeo, but you had no right to treat Angie the way you did."

Chance tightened his hand on Casey's. "What right did you have to fall in love with her?" he threw at Kyle. "She was my wife, Kyle. *My wife!* You had no business loving her."

The force of his emotion coursed through him and into Casey. She didn't blame Chance for being angry, but after this many years, they had to find a way to put the past to rest.

"Maybe not, but she needed somebody. You sure as hell weren't giving her any attention. You only cared about you. The funny thing was"—Kyle gave a short bitter laugh—"she still loved you. Oh, she'd walk with me, and we'd go riding together, and she'd talk and talk but only about you. That's all there ever was between us, you know. Talk. Nothing ever happened. Not that I wouldn't have liked it. I loved Angie, but she never knew that. I never told her."

Chance shrugged. "I still don't understand. Why did you leave with her?"

Kyle chewed on his bottom lip and stared down at his clenched hands. "I was afraid for her. She couldn't stop crying that day. You and Dad went to some cattle meeting, but she thought you were signing up for another rodeo gig. I couldn't convince her otherwise, and she said she had to leave. I tried to stop her. She was in no shape to drive, but she refused to let me get behind the wheel. So, at the last minute, I jumped into the car. I figured wherever she was going, I'd talk her out of it before we got far."

Kyle grimaced and twisted his fingers together. "It didn't work out that way. Once on the highway, Angie told me she was headed home to her parents' ranch. I wanted to at least see she got there safely, and then I'd hitch a ride back. The storm hit...unexpectedly. Couldn't see a thing. I wanted her to pull over, but she started crying again. She told me you two had argued, but that's all I could get out of her. She wasn't rational. Scottie was asleep in the back seat, and I didn't want to wake him, so I reached over to take the wheel." He halted and swallowed hard, running one hand behind his neck. "She fought me. The next thing, we were sliding...and sliding, and there was a truck jackknifed..." Kyle's voice trailed off, and he buried his face in his hands. "I don't know why they died, and I didn't. I should have. It should've been me instead of them. To this day, I wish I had died." His shoulders heaved.

Marianne put her arms around him, crooning in a soothing tone.

Casey glanced at Chance, who had remained silent the whole time Kyle related the story.

He let go of her hand and flicked a jerky finger beneath his eyes.

Barely able to contain her own tears, she glanced away. Seeing his pain would be her undoing.

Kyle scrubbed his hands over his face. "I blamed myself for the accident. When I got home from the hospital, I wanted to beg your forgiveness, but you split for the cabin. I never saw you show any grief except for Scottie, and then you left the ranch for good. I figured you were glad to be free again."

Chance rose and walked to the big picture window that faced the mountains. Parting the draperies, he stared out into the night. "You were young. You knew nothing of what happened between Angela and me, and you know nothing of what I felt for her. But I tell you this, brother. From the day we met, I loved that woman. I just didn't know how to make her happy anymore. After Scottie was born, she changed. She didn't want to live here, and she sure as hell didn't want my affection. About that time, I started sleeping in the bunkhouse. She wouldn't let me anywhere near her."

"Billie said the doctor told her she shouldn't have more babies," Kyle protested. "That she must've had a hard time."

Chance emitted a bitter laugh. "She had morning

sickness a lot, but we barely got to the hospital when Scottie was born. Angie just got turned off by the whole thing. She told me right then she didn't want any more kids. I said okay, if that's what she wanted, but then she made up a story about the awful time she had giving birth and that she couldn't have more children. I wasn't about to tell everybody she was lying."

What a heartbreaking situation. Casey leaned forward in the chair. *Why couldn't Justin or somebody have helped Chance and Angela figure out what went wrong?*

Kyle rose and paced around the room. "Why did she do that? Angie acted like she enjoyed being a mom....most of the time."

"I don't know, but I suspect she had some other problem. Maybe depression? I wish I'd gotten her some help. She always was a dreamy sort of girl. That's what first attracted me, but she had all these crazy romantic fantasies about what our marriage should be and just couldn't cope with hard realities."

Kyle frowned. "She said she still loved you."

Chance shook his head. "Maybe she did, in her own peculiar way, but for a long time, Angie and I were married in name only. She wanted it that way."

The soughing of the wind in the pines broke the tense silence in the room. Casey shivered at the sudden dampness and, for something to do, she left the chair and laid a small fire in the grate. The warmth of the flames crept outward, dispelling the chill. She turned around.

Kyle stood beside Chance and rested one hand on his older brother's shoulder. A grudging respect born of grief and guilt flickered between them.

How much the two men had suffered these past five years, but maybe they could finally make peace.

"I was pretty young and stupid then, too," Chance admitted. "I didn't know what to do or how to solve our problems, but I never stopped loving Angela...or my son."

Kyle nodded and gripped his brother's shoulder. "I guess we've both been running from what happened. If we'd had this talk years ago, it might've spared us all a lot of pain."

"We've talked now." Chance grabbed Kyle's arm and met his gaze. "Maybe Angie can finally rest in peace."

Later, when the wind died, Kyle and Marianne walked out into the summer night.

Casey sat beside Chance on the sofa and studied the lines of fatigue that etched his face. She longed to put her arms around him and tell him everything would be okay. But maybe for Chance, healing still hadn't begun. She watched him reach into his shirt pocket and draw out a tattered photograph. From the creases, she knew he'd carried the picture a long time.

He smoothed the photo in a loving gesture. "This is Scottie. This is my son." A smile crinkled his face.

Casey leaned closer and gazed down at the picture of a child with dark hair and sparkling blue eyes, a miniature of his father. In the photo, Scottie stood next to Buckwheat, and his boyish smile melted Casey's heart. "How old was he here?"

"I took this on Scottie's fifth birthday, two months before the accident. We had a party for him. Billie made a cake. Sam played his fiddle. I asked Angela to come to the party. She stayed in her room. She had a headache."

Casey rubbed his arm in sympathy for two people who had hurt each other so much. "Maybe she really was sick, Chance."

"Yeah, but he was just a little boy. She could have—I don't know—made the effort. She should have tried." Chance drew the harmonica from his pocket where he kept the photograph. He turned the instrument over and over in his hand, staring at it as if the harmonica could give him some answer. "I used to play this when Scottie was a baby. He cried a lot, and the music soothed him. When he got older, he just liked to hear me play." His voice stilled, and he clenched his fingers around the harmonica. "She should have left him here the day she ran from the ranch. If I'd been home, I could've stopped her, but I was off with Justin, buying some damn cows. Because ranch business was so important, and I was trying to be the man of the family. I thought that's what I was supposed to do. But it cost me my son. I failed him, Casey. I failed to keep that little boy safe."

Casey pressed a finger beneath her eye to stop a tear. "You couldn't have known what would happen or what Angela would do."

Chance still gazed at the photograph. "Angie grew up on a ranch. I figured she'd be okay with this life. I was wrong…or maybe she just couldn't live with me. I tried to be a good husband and father. It just wasn't enough for her."

"I think Angela had more going on than anyone realized. No one is to blame for what happened, any more than for what happened to Matt. But you need to forgive your brother and Justin and Angela. Most of all, you need to forgive yourself. I think Scottie would want you to do that." Last night, as she'd watched Chance sleep, a million different emotions had drifted through her mind. She wanted to make his life better and help him heal. Perhaps then she would heal, too.

The fire burned down in the grate, and the minutes ticked by on the mantel clock. Casey waited for him to speak.

Chance leaned his head on the back of the sofa and closed his eyes. "I didn't want to forget Scottie. I was afraid if the pain went away, I would forget. I thought if I came back to the North Star, I'd find a way to live with the past. I don't know if I have, but with your help, Casey-honey, I'll keep trying." He opened his eyes and tilted his head. "Come here."

She curled into his arms and buried her face in his shoulder. Just touching him now eased the stress of the evening, and she welcomed his familiar warmth. But so many ups and downs had taken place over the summer. Would life with Chance always be this way?

He kissed the top of her head. "I'm sorry you had to hear all this tonight."

"It's better I did." She lifted her face. "Now, I understand why you left the valley and stayed away so long. I know it's something you won't do again."

"Not as long as you're here." He hugged her and dipped his head to kiss her long and slow. "Are we still talking wedding?" he murmured against her lips.

She ran her fingers through his tousled hair. "Yes, we are. As soon as Justin comes home. Maybe we can get married in that little chapel by the Snake River."

"Whatever you want. Wherever you want, I'll make my promises to you."

Casey couldn't wait for them to make those promises and tugged him closer, sealing tonight's promise with a kiss that sent her heartbeat into overdrive. The man really did know how to kiss. She'd never tire of feeling his lips on hers.

Chance leaned away and brushed her hair back from her face. "Will you go with me tomorrow to see Justin? I've got to check on the surgery plans and convince Billie to come home. I'm not sure she'll listen."

"Of course, I will." In her heart, Casey knew Justin's illness was just the beginning of tough times ahead. But whatever came about, she'd stick it out here in the valley.

Chapter 21

At breakfast, Casey asked Roy if he would look after Jamie while she visited Justin. "I told him to behave," she assured him. "He's in the barn with Buckwheat."

"I'll keep him busy. He won't be any trouble." Roy had stayed after the others left for the day. He stood in the kitchen, drinking another cup of coffee.

"If he acts out—"

"He won't." He leveled his gaze at her. "Hey, no problem, Ms. Casey. He can help me feed a couple of calves we're weaning." He drained the cup and set it on the counter. "Good stuff, your coffee. Been keeping us going since you got here." He gave her a teasing grin, but a calming light glittered in his dark eyes.

After the tension of the last twenty-four hours, Casey relaxed a little. "So I've heard. You need more?" She lifted the large glass pot from the coffeemaker.

His gaze passed over her once more but darted away when footsteps sounded in the hall. "No thanks." He held up a hand. "Got work to do."

"I'll take some." Chance entered the kitchen, buttoning the cuffs on his shirt. "You ready to go? I told Billie we'd be there in an hour." He stopped and glanced between them. "Everything okay?"

The wrangler grabbed his hat and settled it on his head. He reached for the doorknob. "Sure enough."

Before leaving, he turned to Casey. "Give the boss man our best. We're all rooting for him to get home quick." He opened the door and shut it quietly behind him.

Chance took the mug Casey offered. "What was that all about?" He sipped the potent brew.

Casey flicked the off switch on the coffeemaker. "I just asked Roy to keep an eye on Jamie while we're gone." She grabbed a notepad and pen on the counter and dashed off a message—*sandwiches in the fridge for lunch*—and propped it against the cookie jar. "I'm sure they'll find it there." She picked up her purse and slung the strap over her shoulder. "Let's go."

Chance gulped the rest of his coffee and followed her but stopped at the door. "Roy's a good guy. I trust him."

But did he trust her? That was the conundrum. Casey paused and lifted her chin. "He is, and he's a good friend. My friend. Nothing more, Chance."

"I know. It's just…" His eyes flickered with an old light of anguish.

Casey read their silent question. Even after everything had come to a head, the history of Angie, Kyle, and himself still haunted Chance. Would his sense of distrust stand between them? She stepped closer and laid her hand on his chest. "It's you and me, from now on, cowboy. You need to believe that with your whole heart."

He nodded and followed her out the door.

She climbed into the pickup. "Will your brother visit Justin today?" After all that had transpired last night, was Kyle okay?

"There's a lot of work to catch up on. He'll go later." Chance slid behind the wheel and paused. "It's a fact of hard reality here, Casey—maybe what Angie couldn't accept—in bad weather, on holidays, and even during illness, ranch work continues, and somebody needs to boss the crew."

"Not so different from my parents' farm." As they rolled down the long driveway, Casey stared out the truck window. The wildflowers in the valley were fading, a sign of the coming autumn. In the pale-green summer pasture, a small herd of bison grazed. The beasts were a part of the new life she must accept by marrying Chance, along with wild rivers and snow-capped mountains. How would she learn to deal with so much change? *Maybe by letting go of the past.* The sooner they both did that, the sooner they could move on.

Chance turned the pickup onto the highway that a few months ago had led him home. A little farther on, he reached across the seat and grasped Casey's hand. "It was my lucky day when I stopped in that café in town. You know that, don't you? I wasn't certain about coming home, and if you hadn't given me a ride, I'm not sure I would've made it the rest of the way."

Casey rubbed her fingertips over his work-worn hand. "You would have, because you needed to. Now, Justin needs us to do whatever it takes to keep the North Star going. That means you and Kyle getting along and working together." *And trusting me.*

"Yes, ma'am, Ms. Casey." He nodded and sent her a wink.

They kept their visit with Justin short. He would have surgery within a few days. Outside the ICU, Casey noticed the gray shadows beneath Billie's eyes. The woman was exhausted. "You better come home later with Kyle. We don't need two of you sick."

Billie nodded and glanced from Casey to Chance. "Am I right if I say you two have figured things out?"

Chance held Casey's hand and lifted it to his lips, kissing the back of her fingers. "You usually are right, Billie. From as far back as I can remember, you were right about a lot of things."

She hugged them both. "Your daddy will be happy to hear this. Is it okay if I let him know? It'll give him a reason to get through this surgery and come home quick as he can."

"Sure," Casey said. "Tell him he has a wedding to attend and a book to finish, and that I'll be around to help him with it." What her own family would think of her decision was anybody's guess.

On the way home, Chance turned onto a side road and drove into the hills. The dirt two-track twisted and turned and finally ended high above the valley with a view of the Buffalo Fork River running through the pastures. He stopped and motioned for her to get out.

"What is this place?" Casey followed him to the edge of the ridge. Below them, the river meandered past evergreens, scrubby brush, and the willows that were taking on their autumn hues. A long-legged moose and her calf browsed on the bank.

Chance took off his hat and glanced around the clearing. "There was a spot I came to as a kid. When I argued with Justin and went out riding, I always ended up there. Like it drew me, and I belonged in that place."

"Is this it?" Casey lifted her gaze at a sharp cry. Above them, an eagle sailed on the air currents in graceful flight. "It's a beautiful spot. I can understand why it drew you."

"No, it's not the same, or maybe I just imagined how it looked. You know how kids are. They like their secret places, even if they're not real. It's been a long time since I searched."

Casey put an arm around Chance's middle and hugged him. "But I think that place is real, and you'll find it again."

He drew Casey closer and tucked her against his side. "Doesn't matter. I found you. That's all I'll ever need."

Casey watched the eagle disappear into the vast blue sky. "Is his mate out there somewhere?"

"I'm sure. Eagles mate for life, you know."

A deep sense of commitment filled Casey's heart. Much like Martha McCord did in the past, she would face whatever came their way. "I can't wait to tell Jamie we're staying here. I know he can't replace the son you lost, but you can be the father he needs. We'll have a good life." That earned her a kiss on the cheek.

The sun cast a golden light over the Tetons, and the rays caught the cascading motion of some distant waterfall, sending up a prism of light much like a rainbow. The sight reminded Casey of that first day Chance had hitched a ride home to the North Star. She pointed toward the elusive arc of color. "I think the rainbow is a sign telling me I'm supposed to be here." The colors faded in the sunlight, but she hoped what she felt today would never fade.

Chance turned her to face him. "So, I guess there is one, after all."

"One what?" Casey moved her gaze from the mountains and focused on the love shining in his deep-blue eyes. She would never tire of looking into them.

"A rainbow's end." He drew Casey into the circle of his arms.

"Where dreams come true." She stood on tiptoe and locked her hands around his neck. Leaning into him, she savored a warm rush of anticipation. "But it's not endings I'm thinking about right now."

He tipped his forehead and touched hers. "What are you thinking about?"

"Only beginnings," she whispered. "Only many sweet beginnings."

High above the valley with its winding river, the Wyoming wind blew past and carried her words to the mountains beyond. When the wind rushed back, Casey heard a single whispered word: *home*. Had the mountains themselves spoken? Perhaps, but all that mattered was the adventure that lay ahead.

Chance bent his head and kissed her.

She sank into his embrace and gave up her heart to a new future. Later, she would tell him about the lifetime they'd spend learning about rainbows and promises and love.

A word about the author...

Lucy Naylor Kubash has had a lifelong love of reading and has been writing for as long as she can remember. She is published in short fiction and novel length contemporary romance, as well as nonfiction, having written a column called the Pet Corner for over twenty years. She is a member of Michigan Romance Writers, Grand Rapids Region Writers Group, Romance Writers Online, and Women Writing the West. She loves anything to do with the American West and especially traveling there whenever possible. When not writing she likes to spend time with her family and pets. www.lucynaylorkubash.com

Other Titles by this Author
The Haunting of Laurel Cove
Will O' the Wisp